Sweet & Rich

A SWEET WATER NOVEL

SAMANTHA WHISKEY

D1714198

Also by
Samantha Whiskey

Briggs

Caspian

Brogan

Maxim

The Raleigh Raptors Series:

Nixon

Roman

Hendrix

The Onyx Assassins Series:

Crimson Covenant

Crimson Highlander

Crimson Warrior

Crimson Truth

Crimson Kiss

Crimson Hunter

A Modern-Day Fairytale Romance:

The Crown

The Throne

Now Available in Audiobook!

CAROLINA REAPERS SERIES
Spicy southern nights meets the chill of the ice in this hot hockey romance series!
Axel
Sawyer
Connell
Logan
Cannon

SEATTLE SHARKS SERIES
Let the Sharks spice up your commute!
Grinder
Enforcer
Winger
Rookie

ROYAL ROMANCE SERIES
These twin princes are sure to help you escape!
The Crown
The Throne

For those who always love us for exactly who we are

CHAPTER 1

Luna

Me: I can't do this.

    Zoe: Yes you can. Wait. What are you doing?

    I blew out a breath, my fingers shaking as I texted my best friend Zoe.

Me: I'm in Dennis's apartment, waiting for him to come home from his trip.

Zoe: That seems like a very easy task to accomplish.

I glanced down at what I was wearing, and cringed.

Me: I'm wearing fishnets. And garters. And a bra that barely covers anything.

Zoe: Damn! Get it!!

I laughed, the action helping ease some of my nerves. Dennis and I had been dating since my freshman year in college—so just over five years. I shouldn't be nervous at all... except, I *was*.

It could be the fact that Dennis constantly made me feel *less* than adequate in the bedroom, but I'd always chalked that up to him having more relationships in high school than I did. I mean, when we did have sex, we made it work. It wasn't mind-blowing or anything like it was in the books I read, but it was something we did as a couple. Something that signified the intimacy in our relationship.

I just wanted it to happen more. I wanted to experiment to see if we could have that spark that was always present in my favorite romance novels. Any time I'd come to him with a scene from one of the books I was reading, he'd tell me it was a fantasy and that real life would never live up to those expectations. And, I suppose, he wasn't wrong. I'd never had an orgasm from just his hand or his mouth, and that happened like a zillion times before chapter twelve in almost every book I read.

Plus, he was the only real boyfriend I'd ever had. Dennis was my first, and since he had more experience than me, I'd always let him take the reins.

But things had been strained between us for a while and I was looking to shake things up. I hoped he'd see me sprawled out on his couch with this outfit on and not be able to keep his hands off of me.

Me: Am I crazy?

Zoe: Are you asking me as your best friend or as your best friend who happens to be a clinical psychologist?

Me: I wouldn't say no to Dr. Casson's opinion on this one, but throw in a little bit of my friend too.

It was both a blessing and a curse having Zoe as a best friend—we'd known each other since high school—and while I loved her brilliant mind and the way she broke things down for her patients, I understood it was hard for her to turn off when it came to girl talk. But bless her, she always tried for me.

Zoe: You need a change.

Me: In what way?

Three little dots popped up on our text, then went away, then came back again. My heart sank. Zoe wasn't Dennis's biggest fan, and Brad downright hated him. Both my best friends had expressed many times that I deserved better, but they didn't know Dennis the way I did. He could be kind, charming even. There were times he really tuned in and made me feel like we were the only two people in the world.

Or at least he had been in the beginning.

Lately he'd been short with me, constantly criticizing the amount of time I was putting into my little boutique and my dreams of starting my own clothing line. But that just meant we'd hit that age-old relationship rut, right? All we needed was something to mix it up and we'd get back to where we started.

Zoe: It means that you need your emotions and feelings to be heard. And he needs to change in order to do that.

Me: Okay, that was Dr. Casson. Now be Zoe.

Zoe: He'd be crazy not to drop to his knees and worship you the second he sets eyes on you.

I smiled brightly at my phone, a thrill rushing through me. I didn't need him to worship me, I just wanted some emotional and physical attention. I was practically starved for it with how distant he'd been recently. And it wasn't like I hadn't been putting in the effort on my end—I tried to create fun dates for us, tried to create the quality time that laid all the ground work for intimate time as well. But for so long now, he'd been rushed, pushy, or too tired to give me time at all, quality or intimate.

Me: Maybe I'm trying too hard.

Zoe: Maybe you shouldn't have to try so hard.

I swallowed a lump in my throat as I read her response. Maybe I was trying to ignite something that had fizzled out. Maybe Dennis would never see me as the sexual being I felt like. Maybe he'd never *try* with me. And that's all this was about, me asking him to try. If we ended up not enjoying being a little wilder in bed, then no harm no foul, right?

Zoe: I love you, babe. I think you're amazing. If I walked in on you like that I would tear you to pieces.

I laughed out loud at that one, the well-timed joke shoving all the doubt out of my head.

Me: Same. He's ten minutes out. Wish me luck.

Zoe: You don't need it!

I double-checked the find-my-phone app we'd set up on each other's phones after a year of dating, and nodded to myself before setting my phone on the end table next to the couch. He was close, and with each minute that ticked by my heart raced a little faster.

It was cold in here, raising chill bumps all over my exposed skin, and I switched my position about a dozen times. What was more flattering, one leg up and on the back of the couch, my spine pressed against the cushions and chest sticking up? Or was it me sitting up straight, legs spread so he could get a full view of the entire outfit?

There wasn't much to it—scraps of lace and fishnet, with black triangles of fabric barely covering my nipples. If I would've planned ahead, I would've made something for myself, but I'd been spontaneous in this choice. Dennis had been out of town for work for a week, and we hadn't made plans to see each other tonight, but I thought a sexy surprise might be just the thing to treat us both for his return home.

Dennis's voice sounded from outside the front door, which was directly across the room in his quaint apartment. He must be on the phone, which only made my heart climb up my throat even more. If he was on a business call, then he definitely wouldn't be happy about the shock—

The door swung open, and Dennis stumbled inside...

With another woman in his arms.

My heart plummeted to my stomach, my entire body freezing where I sat, legs spread wide on his couch.

He was kissing her feverishly, his hands roaming over her entire body. He looked passionate and invested and—

"Um..."

Um? That's what came out of my mouth? Fucking hell.

They broke apart at the sound of my brilliant outburst, Dennis's eyes flaring wide when he spotted me.

"Who the hell is she?" the woman asked, her brow furrowed as she took in my appearance.

Kill. Me. Now.

My mind finally caught up with my body, and I grabbed the throw from the back of the couch, wrapping it around my shoulders. It was small so it only covered my top half, but I'd take it.

"Luna," Dennis said, his mouth practically gaping open. "What the hell are you doing here?"

He could've smacked me and I would've been less shocked. "That's your response?" I asked.

"Omigod," the woman said, and to her credit, she looked absolutely mortified. "Are you dating him?"

"Yes," I said.

"For how long?"

"Five years," I answered, my heart shattering at the way Dennis stood there looking between us during our exchange. From the way he ground his jaw, he was angrier about getting caught than he was worried about hurting either one of us.

"*Ew,*" she said, raising her hands and taking a giant step away from him. "Girl, I had no idea. I promise. I'm so sorry."

I raised my brows at Dennis, waiting for any sort of response.

"You're an asshole," the woman said before stomping out of the door and slamming it behind her.

He really was.

I'd been trying, hadn't I? I planned dates and cooked him meals at home when he didn't want to do the dates I planned. I'd laugh at his jokes and go to his business functions. I even loaned him money when he was struggling. I tried. I *really* fucking tried.

"Are you really going to stand there and not say anything?" I finally snapped once the anger had replaced most of the mortification.

"Don't." He shook his head, jerking his tie from around his neck. "You shouldn't even be here, Luna—"

"Are you kidding me?" I cut him off, shaking my head before hurrying into his bedroom where I'd left my bag.

He followed me inside, hovering in the doorway. "You aren't!"

"And you weren't supposed to be fucking someone else!" I fired back, grabbing a pair of sweats out of the bag and shoving my legs inside them.

"You don't understand," he said.

"Please, explain it to me!" I shook my head, dropping the throw and pulling a T-shirt over my head. "God, I'm such an idiot. Sitting here hoping you'd love this," I mumbled to myself, gesturing at the lingerie that was now thankfully covered up by my usual clothes.

"This isn't like you," he said as I hoisted my bag onto my shoulder. "Is this a stunt from one of those ridiculous books you read?"

My mouth dropped as I looked up at him where he was blocking my path. "You're unbelievable." I sucked in a sharp breath. "How long?"

"How long what?"

"How long, Dennis? How long have you been cheating on me? How long have you been pushing me away when I try *anything* intimate with you, while you've clearly been welcoming whoever the hell that was into your arms without a second thought?"

He had the audacity to look annoyed.

Wow.

Had he always been this heartless? This cold—

"You have no idea what it's like being a man," he said. "*None.*"

Anger licked up my spine. "Enlighten me."

"We have needs that can't be satisfied by one woman," he said, reaching for me. "You know how I feel about you, Luna. You're great. There are just things I can do with her that I can't do with you."

I jerked away from his touch, revulsion rippling through me. Tears gathered in the back of my eyes. "I've been asking for more…" I shook my head. It didn't matter. He clearly didn't see or want me in that way. "Five years. You told me you loved me—"

"I do love you," he cut me off, reaching for me again. I backed up, and he raised his hands like he was trying to calm a wild animal. "I do. Maybe it's a good thing this happened."

"Are you fucking kidding me?"

"I don't want to hide from you anymore. If you can accept that I need multiple—"

"No," I cut him off. "You can stop right there. You barely entertained my ideas when it came to sex, so no, I won't be *understanding* your need to find pleasure in other partners. We never agreed to anything like that. God, you always lose your shit when I have lunch with Brad and he's my best friend—"

"He's an asshole," Dennis said.

"That's rich, coming from you." I tried to move past him, but he blocked my way.

"Don't be like this, Luna," he said. "Tons of people have open relationships—"

"Yeah," I said. "And the thing about those relationships? They set up those rules and boundaries beforehand. They don't lie and cheat and *hurt* each other."

"It's cute that you think you know a thing about it," he said, and I cringed at the level of arrogance in his tone. "Luna, you've depended on your trust fund your entire life. You have no idea what the real world is like."

I gaped at him. I built my boutique from the ground up, using money I'd earned by selling custom pieces...actually, fuck this. "Get out of my way."

"No," he said, folding his arms over his chest. "Not until you calm down. You're being irrational."

I took a deep breath, letting it out slowly. At least I didn't have the urge to cry anymore. Now all I wanted to do was punch him in the throat.

"Move out of my way. Now."

"Or what?"

Unease shot through me. I'd never been afraid of him before, but he was trapping me here. Adrenaline replaced every other emotion, and I quickly shoved past him, racing into the living room where I left my phone.

He raced behind me, stopping in front of the door. "You're not leaving until you talk this out with me."

"There is nothing to talk out!" I snapped, finally getting my phone. "We're done. You cheated on me. You betrayed me. You...you're a liar. And I'm done."

"Luna," he said, drawing out my name like he was talking to a child. "Nothing has to change between us—"

"Everything has changed!" God, he was making me feel like I was the one losing my mind. "We're done. It's over. Let me leave."

He remained standing in front of the door, and every instinct in my body flared with warning.

I pulled up 9-1-1 on my phone, my thumb hovering over the call button.

"The cops?" he asked, glaring at me. "You're seriously going to go there? Don't you think you're overreacting—"

"Move or I call them."

He rolled his eyes, but stepped out of the way.

Relief spiraled down my spine and I sprinted out of the door, racing down the steps until I reached the parking lot and my car.

He called after me, but I ignored him, driving away as quickly as possible.

It wasn't until I stepped inside my house that the adrenaline faded and the tears hit me.

I dropped my bag and slid to the floor, leaning against my closed front door, not having the energy to take two more steps inside. Tears streamed down my cheeks, hurt, angry tears as memories and emotions whirled inside me. Every time he'd told me he wasn't in the mood, every time he'd told me he was too tired to go out, every time he'd ignored one of my polite requests for something different.

He didn't care about me or my feelings, my needs.

He never loved me.

How could he? Or was I really that old-fashioned to value monogamy in a relationship? I didn't fault anyone who wanted an open relationship, but that just wasn't me. He knew that, and what he'd done wasn't open. It was a lie.

I rubbed my palms against my face, forcing the tears to stop. I wasted years of my life on someone who never even loved me in the first place. How could I have been so—

My phone buzzed next to me, jolting me out of my thoughts. For a second I was terrified it was Dennis, armed with more painful words about how I was the one being ridiculous.

But it wasn't. It was Brad.

I'd never declined a call from my best friend, and I wasn't about to do it just because one asshole ruined my day.

"I know you're going to say no," he said before I even said hello, and something about his voice slid over me like a warm blanket. He'd always been a constant in my life, a source of happiness when everything else was changing. "But the retreat is a week away—"

"Yes," I blurted over him, sitting up straighter.

He'd been asking me for two weeks now to go with him to some corporate retreat hosted by a company he was trying to land. I'd said no, naturally, because I knew Dennis wouldn't approve of it, especially since Brad wanted me to pretend to be his girlfriend the whole time so he could participate in all the couple events.

"You'll do it?" Brad asked, elation coloring his tone. "Really?"

"Yes," I said again, something settling inside me. "A vacation is exactly what I need right now."

"You're the best!" he said, then paused for a second. "What's wrong?"

"Nothing."

"You're lying," he countered. "I can hear it in your voice. What's up?"

"I don't want to get into it right now."

"Fair," he said, and I blew out a breath. God love this man. He never pushed me. "Tomorrow?"

"Sure," I said.

"Lunch. Lyla's Place? We can talk."

"Sounds good."

He hesitated a few beats longer. "I can stay on the line with you," he said. "If that's what you need. Or I can come over."

Tempting. It was so very tempting to have him or Zoe come over and let me cry and vent about the unfairness of it all, but right now, I just wanted to be alone. Plus, I was still wearing the most revealing lingerie I'd ever worn beneath my sweats, and Brad definitely didn't need to see that. A flush raked my skin with just the thought, and I shook my head against my phone.

"Thanks," I said, picking myself up off the floor. "I'm okay. I'm just going to take a shower and go to bed."

"All right," he said. "But if you change your mind I can be over there within ten minutes."

A soft smile shaped my lips at his gesture. "I'm good," I said before thanking him again and ending the call.

I wasn't good.

Because while I was upset and angry, I felt...indifferent.

I felt more unhinged about the things I forgave or over-looked in the relationship than I did about Dennis cheating on me. I felt sad about trying so hard for someone who clearly didn't think I was worth trying for. I felt ridiculous for begging for attention from someone who apparently didn't respect me at all.

I wasted years of my life on him, constantly catering to his needs in the hopes that he'd find time to focus on mine.

Well, I was done trying.

I was free.

Getting out of town for a couple weeks sounded like the absolute perfect prescription to this mess. And who better to do that with than my best friend?

CHAPTER 2

Brad

"There she is," I said, rising from the two-top table in the back of *Lyla's Place* once I spotted Luna heading my way.

Fuck, she looked as gorgeous as ever in a pair of hunter green slacks and a white blouse that she no doubt made herself. Her long red hair hung over her shoulder in fiery waves, and her eyes were bright, but I could see a hint of purple beneath them like she hadn't slept all night or worse, she'd been crying.

"Hey, Brad," she said, her voice off in a way only someone with years of memorizing her tones would notice.

I wrapped her in a quick hug, frowning over the top of her head when she held on to me a little tighter and longer than normal. Reluctantly, I released her, and we settled at the table.

"What happened?" I asked the second she was seated.

She shook her head as she hung her bag over the back of the chair. "Am I that obvious?"

"Only to me," I said, tension coiling in my gut.

"Hey, you two!" Anne said as she came up to our table. "What can I get you today?"

I smiled up at the newest friend to enter our circle—Anne VanDoren, the daughter of Harold VanDoren, a family friend who had tried really hard to set us up recently. Luckily for me, Anne was on the same page that we were better off as friends. Besides, the longest standing relationship—albeit friendship—I'd had with a woman was sitting across the table from me, ordering a lemonade and doing her best to hide whatever was bothering her from Anne.

I ordered a sandwich, Luna copying me with little thought, and Anne headed off shortly after.

"Tell me." It wasn't a request or a demand, it was fact. We shared everything, we always had.

Luna blew out a breath, hesitance shaping her features.

Fuck, it was bad. She rarely hesitated to vent when I gave the opening.

"Dennis and I broke up."

Shock jolted through my body, and it took everything in my power to not smile and try to high-five her. That would be a dick move, but that guy had never treated her right.

"When?" I managed to ask instead of doing a celebratory dance. She was clearly hurting over the situation, and that's the absolute last thing I ever wanted.

"Last night," she said, thanking Anne when she came back with our drinks before leaving to check on her other tables.

"And?" I asked, practically begging her to continue.

Luna had spent her entire college career plus a year being loyal to a fault to that douchebag, seeing something in him I never did. I spotted his narcissistic tendencies faster than Zoe, and that was saying something, since she was the psychologist after all. But any time I brought it up, Luna shut me down. Said I didn't know him like she did.

And maybe I didn't, but I did know one thing—Luna deserved to be treated like a fucking *queen*. Something he never got close to doing.

Luna took a long drink of her lemonade, clearly stalling. "He was cheating on me."

"What?" I snapped.

"Yep," she said, shrugging. "I was waiting for him in his apartment last night," she continued, her cheeks flushing red. "As a surprise. Joke's on me, because he surprised me by walking in with another woman."

I opened my mouth to go off, but she continued.

"To be fair," she said. "The other woman didn't know and stormed off. Then he tried to say it was my fault because I didn't understand the needs of a man." She rolled her eyes. "And then tried to keep me there until I was in a rational mindset to talk about it."

"The asshole wouldn't let you leave?" My hand curled into a fist where it sat on the table.

"Only until I threatened to call the police."

"I'm going to fucking kill him," I said, pushing away from the table, my mind one-tracked and ready to introduce his face to the nearest curb.

"Brad, please," Luna said, her hand darting out to catch mine.

Her touch was about the only thing that could draw me back to the table. I sat back down, doing my best to *breathe*.

"I would've come there," I said.

"I know," she said. "I almost dialed your number instead of pulling up 9-1-1. But I didn't want you to get involved."

"Luna, he hurt you." I furrowed my brow. "I'm involved."

Anne showed up with our food, and flashed me a knowing look. I smiled and waved her off, knowing Luna would fill her in another time if she was ready. They were newly friends, and I wasn't about to spill Luna's situation when it wasn't mine to spill. Anne nodded, somehow understanding before heading off again.

"It's fine," Luna said after taking a bite of her lunch. "Honestly, I'm more mad that I didn't see it coming."

"What?" I usually prided myself on my conversation skills but I was seriously fucking lacking at the moment. Thanks can go to the asshole who broke her heart and my insatiable need to hurt him over it.

She shrugged again, acting like none of this was a big deal even though I could see it was tearing her up. "There were signs," she said. "Signs I overlooked because I thought..."

"Thought what?" I asked when she didn't continue.

"Thought he loved me." Her voice cracked over the last part, and my heart ached for her in that moment. She was the best person I knew. She didn't deserve this. "I thought we'd just hit a rough patch, like all relationships. Especially when every time I asked for—"

She abruptly stopped herself, studying her sandwich a little too intently.

"Every time you asked for what, Luna?" God, I wasn't used to having to pull answers from her. Things between us had always been easy, effortless, so why was she choking up now?

She took a few more bites of her lunch, and I reluctantly did the same, wanting to give her all the time she needed to talk. I know we came here to talk about the upcoming retreat, but fuck that. She needed me to be here to listen, and I would sit here all damn day and night if that's what she needed.

"Let's just say he wasn't very forthcoming in the bedroom recently," she finally said, her cheeks flushing again just like they had when she'd mentioned surprising him at his place. "So last night I bought a silly, skimpy little outfit and wore it and thought it would fix all our problems but instead I ended up making a complete fool of myself, standing there with barely anything covering me while a complete stranger walked in with her mouth all over my boyfriend."

Oh...*oh*.

Fuck, the images that danced through my mind wrecked me. Not only because that situation hurt her in ways she didn't deserve, but in all the ways I couldn't stop seeing what she described. Couldn't stop visualizing Luna in lingerie, eager and ready to greet me when I came home.

I always stopped myself from allowing my mind to wander there even though that's all it wanted to do the last few years. She was my best friend. She meant everything to me, which made the idea of taking my thoughts any further than fantasy terrifying. But there were times—like now—where I couldn't stop my fantasies from playing out.

The ones where I got her all to myself.

The ones where I learned every inch of her body, lingering in all the places that made her breathless.

The ones where her mouth was mine to taste, her body mine to pleasure.

Fuck, I was hard just thinking about it.

"Anyway," Luna said when I hadn't responded. "He constantly told me no when I asked about trying new things. Things that might help me actually..." She shook her head. "Either way, he always said I was living in one of my romance novels and needed to come back down to earth."

"He told you that," I said in utter disbelief. He was fucking lucky to have her in his life, to be able to touch her and love her in that way. She was brilliant and funny and compassionate. How could he ever deny her anything?

"Yeah," she said. "And maybe I was. Those books are a little far-fetched sometimes, but was it so wrong for me to ask for more than something fast with barely any time for me to...never mind."

"No," I said, shaking my head. "It's not wrong at all, Luna. Fuck him. He's a selfish prick who obviously didn't have a clue on how to take care of you."

"Really?" she asked, looking doubtful. "You're a guy."

"Good observation skills," I teased, and it earned me a small smile, thank fuck.

"Right, you're a guy. So forget you're my best friend for a second, okay?"

"That's hard to do—"

"Please, Brad. I'm serious."

"Okay."

"Just be a guy right now and pretend we're dating."

I swallowed hard, but nodded as she dug her phone out of her purse. She clicked a few things on the screen, scrolling before she finally reached a stopping point. She slid the phone toward me, and I scooped it up.

"Pretend we're dating," she said again, her voice lowering. "And I showed you that and asked you if it was something we could try." She nodded to the phone in my hand, the screen covered in text that I could now clearly see was one of her romance books she read on her phone during slow times at her shop, or on her kindle at home.

"I don't know if I'm the best—"

"Please," she said again. "I was up all night trying to figure out if I was reaching. If I really was the irrational woman he said I was. If I was crazy for asking or expecting anything like that. I mean, he said there were things he could do with her that he couldn't do with me, as if he saw me as a non-sexual being. I don't know. It's driving me nuts not knowing if I was overstepping by ever bringing this up."

"Okay," I said, nodding as I turned my attention to the book on the screen, something written by Daisy Lewis. I'd seen that name before, knew it was one of her favorite authors. Fuck, what was this book going to say if Luna thought it could too much to ask for?

I wondered if such a limit existed when I thought about

what she might want, but I couldn't find a justifiable answer, so I focused on the book.

As I read the first few sentences, I completely forgot everything I'd been thinking a moment before. Luna had put me right in the middle of a sex scene between two characters I knew nothing about, but...

It was tame.

It was hot as fuck, but it was tame.

The guy was going down on the girl while she was sprawled out on a kitchen island. I mean, hell, they were just getting started.

I scrolled through the next couple pages, unable to stop myself from searching for the part where it would be a stretch for anyone else to pull off for her.

There was nothing out of the realm of possibility, no intense sex swing or multiple partners or a dom/sub situation that would take days of preparation and boundary setting to accomplish. This book was showing good, consensual sex.

And he'd told her *no*.

He'd told her she was living in a fantasy.

"Fuck," I groaned, unable to keep the word in as I slid the phone back to her.

"Is that asking too much?"

Goddammit, she didn't realize it wasn't. Had he never taken the time to pleasure her just because he could? Had he never taken time with her at all to make sure she was enjoying it?

"Luna," I said, trying my best to find the right words. It would hurt her to realize he hadn't even given her the bare minimum, and I *never* wanted to hurt her. She'd been with Dennis since college. He was her first real boyfriend, so he'd set the standard for her sexually, regardless of what she read or saw in movies. She trusted him to take care of her and he was a fucking selfish bastard who clearly didn't.

"Just tell me," she said, reading my hesitance.

"No," I said. "That's not asking too much."

She nodded, digesting the information. "So, if we were dating and I showed that to you, how would you react?"

I shifted in my chair, fire licking up my spine. "You really want to know?"

"More than anything," she said.

She wanted me to play the role, to do my part in giving her peace of mind on the fact that her ex was an asshole. Well, okay then.

I stood up and rounded the table until I was behind her, one hand on either side of the table as I bent slightly so I could look over her shoulder.

"Show me again," I said, nodding toward her phone.

She quickly opened her phone, the book popping up on the screen. I reached over her, scrolling through the pages again, each time leaning over her just a little bit more until I consumed her space from behind. I could feel the heat from her body, could see the way chill bumps rose on her neck as I dragged my chin over the sensitive area there.

I turned my face, poising my lips at the shell of her ear. "Let's try page eighty-one when we get home, baby," I whispered. Luna gasped a little, the reaction sending another surge of need straight to my dick. "And after that, if you still want more, I'll show you how creative *I* can be."

Luna turned to look up at me, her full pink lips popped open in surprise. Something churned in her eyes, and I held her gaze, allowing myself to live in the role a little longer. Wasn't I asking her to do the same thing with this business trip? Sure, I never thought we'd be discussing the limitations of sexual requests—which wouldn't exist between us if we were together. Fuck, the woman could ask me to drop to my knees right now and I would.

She blinked a few times, her eyes darting from me to my lips and back again. "That's what you'd say?"

I smirked as I nodded, then leaned in again, whispering in her ear. "I wouldn't hesitate to get you off right here, slipping my hand between your legs underneath this tablecloth and seeing how long you could keep a straight face so no one would notice."

Another little gasp, another dent in the armor I kept around my heart when it came to her.

She shook her head like that might help her focus, and then cleared her throat. "Well," she said, and I took that as my cue to sit back down. "You're very good at pretending."

I laughed at that, a bit sadly too. If she only knew how much I wasn't pretending. But she couldn't know. Because she was my best friend, never once showing a hint of interest in me that way, and besides, I'd rather have her in my life in some way than no way at all. And telling her how that offer wasn't me pretending at all would likely send her running. Because who wants to be friends with a guy who also wants to make you come on his tongue?

"And that's good to know," she said. "That he's the jerk. Not me." She shook her head. "I feel like I spent the last five years in a fog. I feel like an idiot."

"Don't do that," I said. "You're amazing, Luna. He's the asshole."

"Right," she said, determination stealing over her face. "Tell me about this retreat."

"We can keep talking about—"

"I don't want to waste another ounce of my energy on him," she cut me off. "Please. I'd much rather focus on this fun trip I'm about to take." She smiled, and it just about took my breath away.

This girl. She was a powerhouse, beautiful and strong and once she set her mind to something there was no stopping her.

"Okay," I said. "It's not going to be like anything we've done before," I admitted. "You've been my date to more galas and functions than we can even count, but this time we'll have to actually act like a couple."

"And why is this one different than the others?"

"Close-to-Custom is a family-owned and operated company," I said.

"The app that lets you take a live picture of yourself and it gives you the most accurate sizes for fashion venues across the globe?" she asked.

"That's the one. They're looking to expand now that they're the number one fashion app across the country. That's why they're allowing investors to bid for their business, but the only time they could have open meetings was during their company retreat."

"And what does me pretending to be your girlfriend do to help you?"

"Like I said, they're a family-owned company. They started off with just two married couples who were all best friends and were tired of buying clothes online that never fit properly despite sizing charts."

"Okay," she said, tilting her head.

"They pride themselves on being partner-oriented, which means they finally started expanding and hiring more people, almost all of whom were couples."

"That's a unique way to do it," Luna said. "But how fun being able to work at a company that supports families."

"Exactly," I said. "Seeing that it's their corporate retreat, they have tons of couple-focused activities where the owners will be in attendance. The other investor vying for them is married, so he'll get a ton of face time with the owners when he brings his wife along."

Clarity hit Luna's eyes. "And you don't want to miss out

on that quality time by not being invited to all the couple stuff."

"Yes," I said. "I've researched the company, the owners, and the employees. They have something healthy here with the potential to go global. I'd be a great investor and would advocate for their brand. I'm not trying to swindle them, I just want a fair shot at giving them my proposal."

Luna sipped from her lemonade, nodding. "I'm in," she said.

I grinned at her. "Even after the game of pretend we just played?" I was half terrified my little role-playing game a second ago would scare her off this idea for good.

She laughed, and the sound skittered along my bones. Fuck, I loved her laugh.

"Yes," she said. "It's not like they'll be asking you to do any of that stuff in front of them." Her eyes flared wide. "Unless it's a completely different type of couples retreat."

"No," I said. "It's all business-oriented stuff, I promise."

She blew out a breath. "Then I think we can pull it off."

"There will most likely be dances, dinners, that sort of thing. We'll have to look like a couple, so I want you to set up your boundaries now so I know not to cross them."

She raised her brows, a wild sort of excitement flashing in her eyes. "We've danced a thousand times before, Brad—"

"Sure we have," I cut her off. "But romantically? The way two people in love would dance?"

"I honestly doubt there is a thing you could do to me in public that would make me skittish," she said, and heat zapped beneath my skin.

I cocked a brow at her. "Really?"

She shrugged. "It's not like you're going to throw me on a table and start worshiping me like in this book," she teased, motioning to her phone on the table.

"Not unless you ask me to," I fired back before I could stop myself.

Her eyes locked with mine, that same sort of charged sensation snapping between us before she laughed again like I'd told her a joke. "Right," she said. "Kissing? Is that a boundary you're talking about?"

I nodded, getting back to business. "I may have to kiss you, if you're not opposed to that, but I'll do my best not to."

Her shoulders sank, and I tilted my head at the move.

"I've been told I'm not very kissable anyway."

"That fucking prick—"

"It's fine," she said, waving me off. "I promise. By the time we go to the retreat in a week, I'll be back to my normal, less-bitter self."

"I don't need you to do that for me," I said.

"I won't be," I said. "I'm doing this for me. I'm just happy you're offering an out. I need a break. And the last thing I want to do is stick around here and wait for him to come to the shop..." Her voice trailed off like she hadn't thought about that until just now.

"If he shows up, just call me," I said. "I'll throw his ass out."

"Who are we throwing out?" Anne asked as she brought us the check.

Luna sighed. "My ex."

"Ex?" she asked, then glared. "Is he crossing lines? You can stay with me and Jim if you need to."

"That's not a bad idea," I said. "Jim is a cop."

Luna laughed. "I'm fine," she said. "I never gave him a key to my place," she continued. "More because he never asked for one, but still."

"Okay," Anne said. "Well, at the very least we're going to do a girls' night out soon."

"I'd love that," Luna said.

"I'll get to work on it." She winked at Luna, taking my card and heading out to ring us up. When she came back, she hugged Luna as we rose from the table, before we headed toward the exit.

"What do you mean there wasn't any seasoning on the rice?" Lyla, the chef and owner of the restaurant, said to Ridge —Jim's best friend and Sweet Water's resident tattoo artist. He had his arms folded over his chest as he looked down at Lyla, who despite being only five foot two, managed to not lose an inch of ground against the giant.

"There's usually green and yellow seasoning in it," he grumbled. "This time there wasn't. I'd like another order."

Lyla shook her head. "That's cilantro and cumin," she said. "And I most certainly put it in there. I made your order myself."

"Make it again."

"I'm charging you," she said, throwing her hands up. "If you don't like that you can find tacos somewhere else."

"I don't want anything for free," he snapped. "I want another order."

"Fine." She waved him off and headed to the seclusion of the kitchen.

"Ridge," I said, nodding toward him as I held open the door for Luna.

"Suit," he fired back.

I rolled my eyes, following Luna out to her car.

"I'll see you soon," I said once she was safely behind the wheel, window rolled down so I could lean against it.

"I'll be around," she said.

"Text me if you need me." I tapped her car and moved back as she started it.

"I always do," she said, waving to me before driving off.

I stood there, staring after her, hating that she was hurting while also selfishly celebrating that I was going to get her all to myself for two whole weeks.

Would it be fake? Absolutely.

Would we have a blast? Definitely.

Was I going to lose my mind trying to keep things strictly platonic between us while simultaneously pretending to be a couple? No doubt.

But none of that meant I couldn't show her a good time, and she needed a good time right now. And I couldn't help it, I wanted to be the one making her feel good, in whatever way she wanted me to.

CHAPTER 3

Luna

I had an hour before closing time and was doing my nightly cleaning routine in the shop when the bell rang above my entrance door. A flash of purple hair was the first thing I saw as I came around the corner.

"Echo!" I said, a smile shaping my lips. I hadn't seen *Scythe's* resident bartender and one of my boutique's biggest advocates in a while. I leaned the broom against the wall and hurried to greet her. "How are you?"

"Fantastic," she said, wrapping me in a quick hug. "I heard through the grapevine that you might need a night out and I have just the thing!"

Apprehension bloomed in my chest. I loved Echo, and we'd been casual friends ever since she opened *Scythe*—our Carolina Reapers' favorite bar—but she was wild where I was more the type to stay in and read a book.

"Don't look at me like that," she said, winking at me before wandering around my boutique. "It's going to be awesome. A friend of mine who owns a club in Charleston is having this epic invite-only masquerade party. Ah!" She stopped when she reached a rack of accessories, selecting a black lacy mask with rhinestones lining the trim. I had an entire section of costume accessories and jewelry that I'd sourced from a vintage shop that closed down a few months ago.

"I don't know if I'm up to that," I admitted, and then tilted my head. "Wait, what grapevine told you about me and Dennis?"

"Oh no, did you two break up?"

I gave her the abridged version.

"Damn, what a dick. Anne only mentioned you needed a girls' night," she said. "I bumped into her at *Lyla's Place* when I was getting my coffee fix."

"Ah," I said, taking the mask from her and heading to the register. I gave her the friends and family discount, even when she told me not to.

"Come on, Luna," she begged after I'd put her mask in a bag. "The Reapers just beat Colorado last night and they have a night off before they hit the road tomorrow. Everyone is going to be there. There will be food and drinks and dancing." She wiggled her hips, an infectious smile on her lips. "Sawyer already got our babysitter," she continued. "I rarely ever take a night off. You have to come. You just *have* to. This will make you forget all about the jerk. Please!"

I laughed at her adorable begging, unable to ward off the electric energy she naturally possessed.

"I guess it's not like anyone will know it's me, right?" I asked, glancing back at the rack of masks. "It might be good for me to step into someone else's shoes tonight."

"Yay!" Echo clapped, bouncing up and down on her feet. "You're the best. I can't wait to hang with everyone tonight. You're going to get busy in this last hour you're open, doll," she said. "I invited *everyone* but it was a last-minute thing, so they're all going to need masks and I told them to come to you."

"You're the best," I said, coming around the counter to hug her one last time before she headed toward the door.

"I'll text you the details!" she called over her shoulder. "Feel free to invite anyone you want! Just text me the names and I'll get them on the list!"

The door swung shut behind her, and I hurried over to the mask rack, grabbing a lacey, hunter green one accented with fiery red gemstones that would go well with my hair. A little thrill of excitement burst through me, chasing all the hesitation away. Why shouldn't I go out and have a good time tonight?

Before, with Dennis, it had always been an absolute chore planning anything. He rarely wanted to go out, claiming he worked too hard during the day and deserved a relaxing night at home. Which, okay, fair, but he also said the same thing on weekends when he didn't work. And if I tried to do anything other than a quick lunch date or dinner with Brad or Zoe? It was a *battle*. Funny, he always accused me of wanting to sneak out on him whenever I went to galas with Brad, and yet he's the one who was actually cheating.

I cringed at the realization, resolving myself to have the best time tonight simply because I *could*.

Me: You're coming to a masquerade party with me tonight.

I fired off the text to Zoe.

Zoe: What? When?

Me: A couple hours.

Zoe: Thanks for the heads up.

Me: I just found out too! Do you need a mask?

Zoe: Already on my way.

I grinned at my phone, pocketing it just as the bell above my door rang again, and a handful of women spilled inside. A few I recognized—like Persephone and Anne—but there were a few others I didn't know.

"Luna!" Anne called, hurrying over to me. "We need help!"

I laughed, waving all of them over to where I kept the masks. "I got you," I said, practically beaming as they descended on my store in a feverish way only friends heading out for a night on the town could.

And I couldn't help it, I loved being a part of it. Sure, I loved the sales that racked up with them buying masks and outfits, but being a part of this community of strong, capable women definitely filled my soul with a much-needed sense of companionship I didn't know I'd been missing.

I rang everyone up, telling them all I couldn't wait to see the outfits put together later tonight, and Zoe walked in right as everyone else was heading out.

She chatted with Anne for a few moments. I knew Anne was one of her patients but they kept a professional and friendly vibe outside of her clinic.

"Did they leave anything for me?" she asked as she came finally came inside, her rich brown eyes wide.

I chuckled, pulling out a glittery silver mask from behind the counter. "I saved the best for you," I said, and she blew out a breath before wrapping me in a hug.

"You're wonderful," she said, squeezing me tight before letting me go. "I'm so proud of you."

"For saving you a mask?" I asked, bagging it without charging her. She tried to protest, but I waved her off. I made the mask and I owned this shop. She was my best friend. Case closed.

"No, for going out tonight. It's a great step forward in learning what your life looks like outside of *him*."

I nodded, grinning at the vicious look she made when she

refused to say Dennis's name. I really had the best friends in the world, and they're support was doing wonders for my soul.

"I'm just glad you were free tonight," I said.

"You know I'm free every night," she said, sighing. "You can thank the string of horrendous dates I've been on urging me to never venture out again."

I laughed. "The last time you went on a date was, what, a year ago?"

"It was *that* bad!"

"Maybe you'll meet someone tonight," I said, waggling my eyebrows at her. "Echo said everyone is going to be there."

She furrowed her brow. "Who's everyone?"

"Reapers, both attached and single, I'm sure. Her friends. Us. Other random people all donning masks to hide their identity. The possibilities are *endless*."

Zoe shook her head. "I'm not even remotely close to hopping back into that dreaded dating pool."

"Neither am I," I said, then pointed to her bag with the mask in it. "But Dr. Casson and Luna Josling aren't going to this party, are they? With the masks, we can be completely different people. Hell, maybe one of us will have a one-night stand that we can look back on when we're older, admiring how adventurous we were when we were young."

Zoe smiled despite herself. "I kind of love this side of you," she said. "Meet you at your place to get ready?"

"Sounds good," I said as she headed toward the door. "I've got twenty minutes and I'll close up shop."

"Love!"

"Love," I called back as the door swung shut behind her.

* * *

Lucid was not only giant, boasting three different stories, a half dozen bars, and private VIP-only rooftop access, but it was packed.

Music blared throughout the space which was coated in muted colored lights that flashed in time to the beats the DJ spun. The thumping rhythm was intoxicating the second the bouncers waved us through the doors. We wove our way through throngs of people dancing in masks, dressed in everything from ball gowns to cocktail attire to fishnets and corsets. It was this beautifully chaotic mixture of fashion that sent my mind whirling with ideas that made my fingers itch for my sketchbook.

But I'd left it at home, having grabbed a Lyft here since I knew both Zoe and I would be drinking tonight, and tonight wasn't about work anyway. Tonight was about pure, undiluted and much-needed fun. Still, I couldn't help basking in the glorious array of fashion happening all around me.

"You made it!" Echo's voice rang out over the music as Zoe and I climbed to the second level, heading to a handful of private lounge sections the Reapers had rented out for the night.

"We're here!" I called back, accepting her quick hug while smiling at her husband Sawyer over her shoulder. He grinned back, looking very dapper in a black suit and mask to match.

A pang of *something* hit me as I waved to the rest of the group hanging out in the booth—which included Anne and Jim, and Persephone and Cannon—among several other couples that Echo introduced us to.

All of their outfits complemented each other, the couples' having clearly planned and coordinated to not double up on colors that another couple was wearing. And not one of the men looked unhappy to be there. Hell, even Cannon, who was terrifying on a good day, was smiling at his wife, both of them wearing glittering blue masks that made them look like the real-life version of Cinderella and Prince Charming.

I hadn't even been able to get Dennis to try a tapas place in Charleston, let alone a full-blown masquerade party.

He didn't think I was worth the work. A weight sank atop my chest, threatening to steal the infectious joy of all my new friends.

But these guys weren't acting like being here tonight was work. They were having a great time, only further solidifying the thoughts in my mind of *if he wanted to, he would*.

Right. He was the asshole. And I was here with people who actually wanted to be around me, who found my company enjoyable. That's what mattered.

I shoved thoughts of him from my mind, settling into a cushioned horseshoe-shaped seat next to Anne and Jim, Zoe flanking my other side.

"I'm so glad we all had the night off," Anne said, clinking her soda water against my cranberry and vodka. "We needed this, right?"

I nodded, smiling at her. She was doing remarkably well, considering we were at a night club with at least half of us having drinks. I knew not all recovering alcoholics would want to put themselves in this sort of environment, but I also was thrilled she wasn't denying herself a good time just because temptation was here. Jim slid an arm around her, the two smiling at each other with that newlywed dust all over them— not that many people knew they'd eloped. I'd been privy to the intel because she bought her dress at my shop.

"Holy shit," Jim said, eyes going wide as a very gruff-looking man wearing a phantom mask approached our table. "You actually came."

I startled slightly as I noticed the man in the phantom mask was none other than Ridge, Jim's best friend and Sweet Water's resident grumpy tattoo artist.

"Figured I might find some new clients here," he said, his tone low and rough as he nodded to whoever he knew in the group.

"Uh huh," Jim said, flashing him a knowing look I didn't understand.

"Has nothing to do with—"

"Can I get by please?" Lyla's voice sounded from right behind Ridge, and it wasn't until he turned around that I saw our favorite Sweet Water chef had just arrived.

Ridge didn't budge, just stood there looking down at her for a few moments that made me shift in my seat with unease. I couldn't tell if he was going to argue with her or if he was going to scoop her up and throw her over his shoulder, whisking her away from prying eyes. Which there were quite a few pairs of single Reaper eyes on her, especially in her stunning white dress and feathery mask that made her look like a freaking angel.

To her credit, she stared right back at him, folding her arms over her chest in defiance.

Finally, Ridge grunted and stepped to the side, allowing Lyla to pass through and take a seat next to Zoe.

"What did I miss?" Lyla asked.

"Not much," Zoe said, motioning to the party. "Dancing. Drinks. It's all just starting."

"Great," Lyla said, selecting a drink from the offering spread on the table before us. "How are you, Luna?"

I laughed softly. "Does everyone know?"

Lyla gave me an apologetic look. "I may have overheard you talking about it at lunch the other day."

I nodded. "I'm fine," I said, and that was mostly true. "I'm actually going on a trip with Brad next week," I said. "I'm really looking forward to getting out of town for a bit."

"Like, *with* Brad with Brad?" Echo asked, having scooted over to hear our conversation. "I've been telling you for a year that you should absolutely climb that multi-millionaire like a tree."

"Babe," Sawyer said, grinning at his wife while he shook his head.

"What?" She shrugged. "I'm not wrong."

I burst out laughing. "He's my best friend—"

"All the more reason the chemistry will be fire," Echo cut me off, taking another sip of her drink.

I waved her off. "I'm helping him out with a business venture," I explained.

"Oh, is he going to invest in your clothing line?" Lyla asked. "I know you've been wanting to put that out on a wider scale for a while."

"No, this is for him," I said. "And he's offered to help me out with the line before, but I don't know..."

My parents were just like the multi-millionaires Echo spoke about a second ago, but that didn't mean I was. I had a trust fund, sure, but my parents didn't exactly approve of the career direction I'd taken. They wanted me to be a doctor or politician. They loved me, but they didn't open the flood gates when it came to support for my business, and they didn't approve of me using the fund for anything other than living situations, education, or charity.

Which was fair, it was their money really. They'd earned it and invested it. But I'd been determined to open my boutique regardless. And I'd succeeded. Now I was making more than enough money to live comfortably without having to dip into my trust fund at all.

"I keep saying you should take him up on his offer," Zoe said, nudging me. "You know Brad never invests in things that aren't winners."

I smiled at them graciously. "I appreciate it. And I have been sketching out and slowly making pieces for a solid clothing line for a while. I just haven't figured out how to put it all together yet."

Dennis said I was reaching too high.

Said my designs wouldn't cut it in the fashion industry because they were too inclusive.

But that was the point of my clothes, to fit all body types and to celebrate all body types. Hell, I had curves for days and sometimes going shopping was an absolute bitch. The best clothes I'd ever worn were the ones I made because they fit my body perfectly. I wanted to offer that on a larger scale, but Dennis had constantly made me doubt my abilities.

Which was stupid, when I thought about it, because what the hell did he know about fashion? God, I'd been so engrossed with making him happy I never once stopped to think about what would make me happy or why he wasn't doing his damnedest to try the same.

"I might," I finally said. "Maybe we'll talk about it on the trip." My response was met with a round of applause I didn't feel I deserved, but I smiled at everyone in gratitude anyway.

"I'm so ready to dance. Who's in?" Anne asked as she stood up, pulling Jim with her.

She was met with a riotous response before almost everyone in the lounge area leaped up and followed her down the stairs toward the dance floor. Even Ridge, who looked like he had a permanent scowl hiding under his mask, slowly trailed downstairs and stood off to the side of the dance floor, intently watching as Lyla, Anne, and Persephone formed a girl dance group.

Our spot on the balcony gave us the perfect view, allowing us to see the Reaper family take over a huge chunk of the space, swaying this way and that to the music.

"You don't want to dance?" Zoe asked.

"I will in a little bit," I said, raising my drink. "Want to finish this first. You go ahead."

"You sure?"

"Yeah, go have fun," I said, urging her on. She winked at me and headed downstairs, easily folding into the Reaper crowd, bumping hips with Lyla.

I watched with an odd combination of pure joy and sadness sweeping through me. I was happy to be included in this little tight-knit group, but another part of me was incredibly sad to not have what most of them did—a healthy, loving relationship that looked fun as hell.

CHAPTER 4

Brad

"I'm glad we could come to an agreement," I said over the phone as I leaned back in my chair, my home office equipped with everything I needed to finish my day here. "With my backing, I believe your condo development will be a real hit in Charleston." I moved some things around on my desk as I wrapped up my last work call of the day, then hung up.

I blew out a breath, that feeling of contentment settling over me like it did whenever I landed another big investment. I'd dabbled in company purchases and sales occasionally, but large-scale real estate was my bread and butter.

I glanced out the windows in my home office, realizing it was already dark. Shit, I'd lost track of time and worked through dinner again.

My phone buzzed on the desk, and I scooped it up.

Luna: I'm excited about the trip and I'm all in. While we're there, maybe we can talk about my clothing line too?

My heart leaped in my chest, an excited buzz rushing through me. Luna had turned down my investment offer for her clothing line no less than ten times. The woman had a talent, and I knew a win when I saw one. But I also understood her position. There was nothing wrong with wanting to stand on her own, but there was also nothing wrong with accepting help either.

Me: Absolutely. We should get a drink and celebrate.

Luna: I'm at *Lucid* in Charleston. Masquerade party with the Reaper fam. Want to come hang?

The visualization that sprinted through my head had me getting up from my chair in a hurry. Luna all dressed up and in a mask no less? I sure as hell wasn't going to miss an opportunity to see her like that. It had been too long since she'd had a proper night out.

Me: I'm in. Be there soon.

Lucky for me, I'd attended more than my fair share of masquerade balls for charity galas in the past, so I had several masks to choose from. I picked one that matched the suit I already wore, and headed out.

After handing my car off to the valet outside of *Lucid,* I was waved in by the bouncer, and stepped into one hell of a party. Music was blaring, dancers were packed on the floor, and the bars were crowded too, but it was more invigorating than overwhelming.

I maneuvered my way through the crowd until I reached the stairs Luna texted me about, and climbed them in a hurry. I stopped two away from the top, the sight of her literally nailing me to the floor.

Even with the mask, I would recognize her by her infectious smile. I'd studied that smile for years, always counting on it to lift even the darkest of days. She wore a dark green, sleeveless dress that hugged her stunning curves, the fabric shimmering in the muted lights of the club. It fit her body like a dream, no doubt a piece she made for just such an occasion, and I was more than blown away. Luna always had that effect on me, not only with her looks, but her passion, her sense of humor, all of it. She was the complete package.

A completely off-limits package, anyway. She was my best friend in the entire world, and if I crossed that line with her and fucked it up? I wouldn't survive losing her in any capacity, so I'd always kept these feelings in check. It had been easier when she was attached to her ex, even if I hated him. At least then I deluded myself into thinking she was happy. But now that she was single? Fuck, it was hard to tamp down the need that blazed through my veins every time I saw her.

She was looking over the balcony railing, not another soul in sight as she gazed down at our group of friends on the dance floor.

"Why aren't you down there with them?" I asked, finally climbing the last two steps and spanning the distance between us.

"I'm having more fun watching," she said, shifting toward me and giving me a quick hug.

I held onto her a beat longer than normal, but managed to stop myself before letting my hands linger on her back. Fuck, she smelled as good as she looked, all notes of lavender and citrus.

"Want a drink?" she motioned to the tables sitting in front of several horseshoe-shaped couches pressed against the back wall of the balcony.

I grabbed one of the soda waters and took a seat, making room for Luna to sit next to me.

"What prompted this evening?" I asked.

"Echo," Luna answered. "She wanted to take me out for a fun night after I told her about Dennis."

"Understandable," I said, and did my best not to clench my jaw. I couldn't help it, every time I thought about what that asshole did to her only made me want to fuck him up even more. I knew she didn't need me to fight her battles, but it didn't stop me from wanting to. "She's a good friend."

"They all are," she said, motioning toward the balcony.

Even though we could no longer see our friends, I knew who she was talking about. Echo, Zoe, Anne, Lyla...all of them. We'd gotten lucky to score such a good group.

"Still," she continued, twirling her drink in her hand. "I kind of wish they didn't know. I feel so ridiculous for not realizing what a jerk he was."

"He's an asshole," I said, the declaration freeing after years of always biting my tongue. "And fuck what anyone else thinks," I continued, dipping my head down to catch her eyes. "You're amazing, Luna. Smart and funny and talented beyond all means. He's the idiot who let you get away. He doesn't deserve it but people should pity him for losing you."

The smallest of smiles graced her lips as she nodded. "He is an asshole," she said, then laughed before taking another drink. "I just wish I didn't feel..."

"What?" I asked when she didn't continue.

She shrugged, setting down her now-empty glass. "I wish I didn't feel like an idiot. Looking back, there were so many signs, and each and every time I either ignored them or convinced myself that it was my fault." She sighed. "My fault that he didn't want to go out on a date with me, my fault that he didn't want to put in an effort for an in-home hang, my fault that he didn't believe in my clothes, my fault that he didn't want to—"

Luna cut herself off abruptly, clenching her eyes shut as she took a visible breath.

"Sorry," she said, opening her eyes again. I hated seeing how much pain churned there, but I could see just as much anger too. "We don't have to keep rehashing this."

"We can rehash it as many times as you want," I said. "Hell, we can dig deeper if you want, or we can pretend like he never even existed. I'll track him down right now and make his life hell, too. All you have to do is say the word."

Luna laughed, the sound trembling all the way down my bones. Fuck, how could a laugh be so sexy?

"We could go put sugar in his gas tank," she said through her laughter.

I joined in, grinning at her. "That was *one* time," I said. "And you know I regret it."

"I don't," Luna said. "Ally deserved it after she cheated on you."

"Yeah, but that was freshman year of high school," I said. "We were kids. It wasn't like we were married."

"Still," she said. "No regrets."

The memory filled me with a sense of nostalgia. Luna never hesitated when it came to me and our friendship, and I'd returned the favor. We had decade's worth of history between us that only fueled how close we were now.

"Sugar in the tank wouldn't be equal revenge," I said.

Luna tilted her head. "What would be?"

Breaking his jaw might do the trick.

"I could buy the company he works for and fire him," I said instead, and a laugh ripped from her lips. "What?" I said, grinning. "All it would take is a call."

She playfully touched my arm, reeling in her laughter. "I guess your revenge flex is a bit bigger now than it was back in high school," she said.

I wet my lips, getting lost in her smile, in how close she sat next to me. "Everything about me is bigger than it was back in high school." The teasing words were out before I could stop them.

Her eyes flared before she nodded. "You were a scrawny thing back then," she teased.

She wasn't wrong, I'd been tall and lanky like a damn bean pole back then. But that all changed in college, where I found

41

weights and cardio and a general love of keeping my body fit and healthy. It was something I learned early on when making my millions—the healthier the body, the healthier the mind.

"Not that I'm one to talk," she continued. "I lived in my paint-splattered overalls and always had charcoal all over my face."

"Some people find that incredibly attractive," I said, my mind whirling and my tongue running away from me. I don't know if it was because of the darkened club setting or the masks giving me this invincible, dangerous feel, but I was having a hard time not going with it.

"Oh yeah," she said. "I had lines of guys begging me for a date. They all were dying to see inside my sketchbook."

"The right one would," I said, and her eyes met mine. Fuck, they were gorgeous, all hazel with notes of green and gold.

"Maybe," she finally said. "Lucky for me I'm not in the market to look for the right one."

"That's good," I said, leaning a little closer. "Especially since you're about to be my fiancé for the next two weeks."

"Does a spending account come with it?" she joked. "I've been eying a new sewing machine for ages."

"We can work that into the deal," I said. "What else do you want?"

She chuckled again, shaking her head. "What am I allowed to ask for?"

"Anything you want," I answered immediately and fucking meant it. She could ask for the world, and I'd find a way to get it for her.

"You can't be this way with all your business deals," she said. "You'd never make any money if you folded so easily."

"I know which deals are worth the effort and which aren't."

"And I'm worth it?" she asked.

I shifted toward her, turning in the seat so I could fully face her. "You're worth everything and more."

Luna visibly swallowed, then laughed. "Then I want dessert every night of this trip."

It was my turn to laugh. "I tell you that you can ask for anything and you ask for dessert?"

"I'm pretty low-maintenance." She shrugged, then arched a brow at me. "So, are you going to give me what I want?"

I studied the lines of her face, the curve of her lips, the subtle way her chest rose and fell as she breathed. Fuck, when did this playful teasing cross over the line to downright flirting? I knew it was my fault, but still. Could she not tell how much of a hold she had on me?

"Always," I finally said, and couldn't help but relish the little bit of shock that flared in her eyes.

CHAPTER 5

Luna

"Dance with me," Brad said, standing up from the couch and offering me his hand.

Hot. Damn.

I didn't know if it was the subtle command in his voice or the playful banter we'd just been having, but flames licked beneath my skin as I looked up at him from where I still sat.

He looked all kinds of regal in a suit so dark green it almost seemed black. A half mask covered his eyes, the same color as his suit, the hunter shade dangerously close to the one I wore.

"Why the sudden urge to dance?" I asked.

"Because this is your favorite song," he said matter-of-factly.

Were those butterflies in my stomach?

"How did you know?" I asked, slipping mine hand in his, grinning as he helped haul me up from my seat before guiding me down the stairs and onto the dance floor.

"I pay attention," he said, spinning me around.

The skirt of my dress twirled before he drew me against his chest, taking the lead as he maneuvered us to the beat of the music. I laughed as I crashed against his chest, but he caught me effortlessly, swaying us to the music with that elegant, smooth way he always had about him.

It *was* my favorite song, one I'd had on repeat for the past few months, and I let the melody fill me as we moved on the floor.

"You look beautiful," he said, blue eyes trailing over my mask to my lips and back again. He gently pushed me out before bringing me back in again, spinning us among the throng of other dancers. "Did I tell you that?"

"You look pretty good yourself," I said, holding onto his shoulders as the song shifted to a slower beat. "Not bad for a fun impromptu night. Beats conference calls and checking the stock market, right?" I teased as we moved to the music.

"Nothing would be as fun as this," he said, one hand sliding behind my back, the other to my hip before he dipped me slightly and brought me back up.

A thrill snapped down my spine at the move, my body reacting to being handled in such a way. I didn't have to worry that he'd lead me the wrong way or drop me or be angry if I accidently stepped on his toes. It was never like that with Brad, it was just...*easy*.

The beat shifted in tempo, a pulsing thrum that I could feel in my bones. Brad grinned, throwing my arms around his neck as he moved us, slipping his massive thigh between my legs, rocking us back and forth in the perfect rhythm.

I laughed, unable to stop the joy swirling around me at the move, giving myself over entirely to the sensation. We were surrounded by friends, old and new alike, and who knew how many strangers, but he made it feel like we were the only two people in the room. That *I* was the only woman in the room, the only one he could possibly want to dance with.

But that wasn't right. Because he was my friend, and it was no secret how well he did with women. The notion threatened to dump a bucket of ice water all over my warm flutters.

"Shouldn't you be dancing with someone else?" I asked despite myself.

Brad furrowed his brow, never stopping for a second. "Why would you say that?"

I shrugged. "There are plenty of beautiful, available women here. I don't want to cramp your style—"

"The only woman I'm interested in dancing with is in my arms," he said, rocking us back and forth for emphasis.

"Are you sure?" I asked, still not wanting to deny him the opportunity to have more fun than he could have with me. "I mean, come next week you'll be stuck with me for two whole weeks."

His grin was pure mischief as he leaned in closer, his lips at the shell of my ear, just like he'd done in the restaurant yesterday. God, that had made me feel things I so shouldn't feel for my best friend, and even now, damn him, it felt *good* to be this close. To have him holding me this way, to smell his incredible earthy scent that reminded me of sage and mandarin.

"Maybe that's right where I want you," he teased, and my heart stuttered in my chest. He stayed right where he was, holding our bodies flush as we swayed to the music.

Heat licked beneath my skin, my body firing with sensation everywhere our bodies touched. We'd danced together countless times before at events or galas, but it had never felt like this. Warmth unfurled in my core the more we moved, and I found myself rolling my hips to the music right along with him. My heart raced, my skin flushing as his hands roamed over me in a possessive way they never had before.

Was he practicing for our little scheme next week? Or was he actually enjoying himself?

No, he couldn't be. This was Brad. He'd never, not once, acted like he was interested in me like that, and besides, I couldn't possibly be entertaining the idea of something with him, right? My body was just reacting to being touched like this, held like this.

Brad spun us again but kept us flush, my breasts grazing his hard chest, making me gasp. God, he felt so good, his hard body aligning with all the soft parts of mine. I clung to him, my eyes fluttering up to his.

Something charged snapped between us as I met his gaze, and I couldn't help it, I looked at his lips and allowed myself to wonder what it would be like to kiss him.

Something shifted in his gaze, and he lowered his head ever so slightly—

We were knocked to the side, someone bumping into Brad's side.

"Sorry, man!" a Reaper said as he righted himself, clapping Brad on the back. Brad waved him off before the Reaper headed off the dance floor.

The shift in view allowed me the perfect glimpse of—

"Omigod," I said, gasping as I whirled Brad around. "Look!"

Brad followed my line of sight. "Looks like Zoe is fully embracing the mask effect," he said, both of us gaping as we watched Zoe being led up the stairs by a tall, dark, and fully masked individual. They didn't stop at the second level or the third either, instead disappearing somewhere near the roof-top access spot.

Brad and I looked at each other, eyebrows raised before we both grinned. "Good for her," I said.

"Hell yeah," Brad agreed. "She needs a little fun in her life, especially with how much she works herself to death. Like someone else I know," he said, nudging me.

"I love my work," I fired back.

"So do I," he said. "But you still have to make time for the fun."

"I am. We're going on vacay, remember?"

"Which is also work for me," he said.

"Not for me. I'm going to indulge in all the perks of being a millionaire's fiancé," I teased.

"Oh yeah?" he asked, pulling me back into his arms to pick up our dance.

"Yep. You already agreed to the dessert clause," I said. "Bring your big bucks because I'm going to eat *everything*."

Brad laughed, holding me a little closer. "Whatever you want," he said, sending me straight back to our earlier conversation when I'd teased him about writing mandatory dessert into our little deal.

He was more than open to anything I suggested and totally supportive, and with the way he was dancing with me? It only made me wonder just how supportive and open he'd be in other areas.

What if I'd asked him for something spicy in the bedroom —if he was my fake fiancé, anyway. It's clear he wouldn't react like Dennis, which had always been fifty shades of judgmental. Brad would never make me feel ashamed of asking for something different.

Maybe it was the drink I'd had earlier or the fun, playful way we'd been chatting before, but I couldn't stop my mind from whirling with the possibilities. It was pure fantasy, since things between Brad and me had never been that way before, but I didn't deny myself the *comfort* I felt right now.

Because that's how he made me feel—there was heat and fire and need too—but *comfort*. Because while Brad and I danced, while I was in his arms, I knew for a fact nothing could touch me. Not the memories of Dennis or the embarrassment I felt over how things ended. Not the unknown of the future or the agony of the present. Here, with Brad, I was *safe*.

Safe to be the truest version of me, and that was more intoxicating than the one drink I'd had.

The beat changed again, but neither one of us moved to leave the dance floor. Somehow, we'd created this magical little bubble that I never wanted to leave. Everything here smelled good and felt good, and I wanted to drown in the sensation of it.

"You know," Brad said, drawing me close to speak into my ear. "This is good practice."

I pressed my cheek against his as we moved to the music, his body flush with mine. "What do you mean?"

"If people are going to believe us," he said, drawing the tips of his fingers down the line of my back. "Then it's good for us to practice me touching you like this," he continued.

Tingles erupted under his touch, causing me to gasp lightly. God, why was my body reacting this way? It wasn't like Brad had never danced with me or held my hand before. But, I supposed he'd never dragged his fingers down my body like that either, and it was innocent. What would it be like if we had to really sell the act and he had to kiss me? How would I react?

"Is this okay?" he asked, his voice low and rough at my ear. He pulled back to gauge my reaction, smoothing his free hand along my cheek and down my neck as we continued to sway to the beat of the music.

"Yes," I breathed the word, my mind and body warring with itself.

He smiled down at me, his blue-gray eyes almost hooded beneath the mask he wore.

"You should probably kiss me," I blurted out the words before my mind could come up with a reason to stop them. "I mean," I continued when his eyes flared wide. "Better here than in a room full of strangers, right? What if I reacted the wrong way and blew our cover?"

"You want me to kiss you?" he asked, almost like he hadn't heard me right before.

"Unless you weren't planning on kissing me during the trip," I answered. "But, if I'm supposed to be your fiancé, I'm guessing kissing will be involved."

Brad wet his lips, something flickering across his features.

Oh, God, I'd somehow ruined the bubble we'd been in—

He shifted, grabbing my hand and weaving us through the crowd of dancers, not stopping until he'd reached a small alcove tucked under one of the balconies above.

"It's fine," I said, my heart racing. "I only meant—"

"You want me to kiss you," he said again, turning to face me. He walked toward me, and I slowly backed up until my spine kissed the wall. Shadows covered his features, the loud thrum of the music vibrating all around us.

"In the name of practice," I clarified. "I'd hate to blow your cover during the retreat."

"Well, then," he said, stepping into my space. He slid one hand over my waist and around me, drawing me flush against him. "In the name of practice," he said before slanting his mouth over mine.

I gasped at the first brush of his lips over mine, the sensation like liquid fire shimmering over every inch of my skin. My hands flew to his chest, fisting the fabric of his suit jacket as I arched against him.

He moved his free hand to my cheek, tipping my head back and sweeping his tongue between my lips in a move so effortless it made my head spin. I opened for him, meeting his kiss with an intensity that matched his as he took my mouth in sweet flicks and dominating licks. My body hummed with sensation, all nerves firing and aching for something just out of reach.

Brad shifted against me, slipping his thigh between my legs as he kissed me deeper. Electricity crackled everywhere our bodies touched, my heart fluttering with every curl of his tongue, every touch of his hands on my skin.

Heat pooled between my thighs, the friction from his muscled thigh pressing into me doing all kinds of things to my body. I forgot everything outside of him—his kiss, his touch, the way he was making me breathless. Everything narrowed to how fucking good he felt against me, around me, his mouth crashing against mine in a feverish hunger that had me questioning every kiss before this.

"*Brad*," I whimpered into his mouth, unable to hold back the breathy little plea.

He pulled back, his chest rising and falling in time with mine. He studied me for a few seconds, his eyes churning with something I couldn't place as he moved away enough to give me space to breathe.

"Looks like you reacted just fine," he teased, grinning down at me.

I bit back a laugh, my mind whirling with what just happened and my body still begging for more. I managed to shrug. "It was all right."

Brad covered his chest with his hands, feigning injury, then shook his head. "Guess, I'll have to do better next time."

Fire licked up my spine, and I stepped up to him, the intoxicating kiss fueling my boldness as I fiddled with his tie. "See that you do."

CHAPTER 6

Brad

Luna sat across from me in her bucket seat on the plane I'd chartered to take us to Myrtle Beach. She was bent over her sketchbook, eyes focused and intent as she dragged a pencil back and forth in a rhythmic pattern that was impossible not to watch.

Her long red hair hung over one shoulder, lightly brushing the edges of her sketchbook as she worked, and her full lips were parted just slightly, her tongue darting out every now and then in concentration.

Fuck, those lips were more than tempting now that I knew exactly how they felt against mine.

Memories of kissing Luna in *Lucid* had consumed me every day since. It'd been five days, but I swear I could still taste her on my tongue, and fuck me, I wanted more.

I *shouldn't* want more, but I'd always had a hard time ignoring my instincts, and now that we'd crossed that line? It was all I could think about. She'd been so responsive, so passionate as she opened up for me, and yeah, we'd said it was all in the name of practice, but it felt like more than that to me.

I'd tried like hell to play it off the second we broke apart, the second I'd felt my control slipping. I had been more than ready to throw her over my shoulder, take her home, and show her exactly how well I could *practice*. But that would change everything between us, and I refused to risk our friendship for one fun night.

You want more than one night.

I ignored the pleading voice in my head, forcing myself to catch up on my emails instead of continuing to watch Luna work—which I could do for hours. There was something so captivating about watching her create works of art on blank sheets of paper.

After an hour of checking and responding to emails, I pocketed my phone, looking over at Luna who was finally taking a break from her work.

"Can I see?" I asked, noting she'd packed away her pencils in the little bag she kept in her much bigger bag.

Hesitation fluttered over her features before she turned her sketchbook toward me. "It's not finished yet," she said. "But I'm getting close."

I took the offered sketchbook, scanning the contents of the pages. "This is your line," I said, recognizing the theme immediately. She'd been working on her own clothing line for years, but this was the first time I'd seen it in a cohesive setting. "This is amazing," I said as I flipped through the pages. "I love that you have the designs on all types of bodies."

"That's my whole vision," she said, excitement flaring in her eyes. "I want to put out a line that is stylish and fun for every type of personality and body. I want it to be fluid too, with no gender labels attached."

"I can see that," I said, dragging my finger along the design of an outfit that could be worn and showcased by anyone. "This is really something, Luna."

"You think?" she asked, biting the corner of her bottom lip. Fuck, I hated the doubt shadowing all of her excitement.

"Yes," I said. "You're working on something that has a wide appeal and it's not only inclusive, but also fun. Empowering."

"Empowering?" She laughed nervously, shaking her head. "I don't know about that—"

"It's all over this," I said, motioning to the sketches. The poses she put the non-descript models in were all powerful and confident. "Your clothes will give people a combination of style, freedom, and confidence."

"Wow," she said, tucking some hair behind her ear. "You really think so?"

"Definitely," I said, handing her back the book. She closed it and tucked in into her giant over-the-shoulder bag. "Why is that so hard to believe?"

She blew out a breath, glancing out the window as the clouds rolled by. "Dennis always said I was reaching," she admitted. "He said that I should be happy I got lucky with my shop and not expect anything more. That I wouldn't appeal to anyone outside of Sweet Water."

I ground my teeth to keep from snapping, and took a deep breath through my nose before letting it out. "You should never settle for anything less than what makes your heart race," I finally said. "Hey," I said, reaching across the space between us and tipping her chin up to mine so she'd meet my eyes. "You shouldn't. Not in life, business, or love."

Her eyes locked with mine, something churning there that I couldn't quite figure out. That recurring tense energy crackled between us, making all my muscles go tight. Fuck, it was like there was a charge in the air and one wrong move would send us up in flames.

"Brad," she whispered my name, almost like a question.

I leaned forward, drawing closer to her—

"We're starting our descent," the captain's voice sounded over the speakers, jarring me back to the present as the flight attendant shuffled down the aisle, ensuring we were buckled in and had everything stowed away.

I settled back in my seat, blowing out a tight breath.

"Thanks," Luna said.

"For what?"

She motioned toward her bag where the sketchbook rested. "For believing in me."

"Always."

The wheels touched down in a semi-smooth landing. I grabbed Luna's bags and stored them in the back of the car that I'd arranged to pick us up, and held the door open for her to climb in the back seat. She arched a brow at me, her gaze darting from me to the opened door and back again.

"What?" I asked.

"Holding the door open for me?" She laughed. "You're already in full fiancé mode, huh?"

I waved her off. "Act like I don't do this for you all the time."

She considered that, almost looking like she was filing through years of history for the evidence. Shrugging, she climbed in, and I slid in after her.

"But yes," I said after we'd gotten on the road. "I am in full fiancé mode as of right now."

"Oh," she said, shifting in the seat toward me just slightly. "Okay, hang on."

She closed her eyes, taking a long, deep breath deep. It was cute as hell.

Opening her eyes, she blinked a few times, her features shifting into a full adoring gaze. She reached across the small space between us, laying her hand on top of mine.

"What are we doing tonight, dear?"

I bit back a laugh, turning my hand in hers so I could

interlock our fingers. "Tonight is the welcome party, darling," I said, having a little too much fun with this charade. "There will be music, drinks, food. It's black tie."

"Good thing I brought all my ballgowns," she said, grinning at me.

"You'd be ravishing in anything," I said. "But I'm glad you packed for the occasion."

"Will there be dancing?" she asked as our car pulled into the beachfront resort we were staying at.

"I'm sure there will be," I said. "Are you ready to dance with me again?"

Luna visibly swallowed, her tongue darting out to wet her lips. The move seemed almost subconscious, like she was remembering exactly what I was remembering—the last time we danced, we ended up in a small, darkened space with my mouth over hers.

A lick of flame snapped down my spine at the memory, and I had to shift where I sat. Fucking hell, I got semi-hard anytime I thought about that kiss.

"Yes," she finally answered. "I think I need way more dancing in my life."

She did. She deserved dancing and fun and adventures and passion. All the best things that life had to offer. She'd been denied those things for way too long—her devotion to opening and running her boutique and then her attention to her relationship had taken up so much of her free time. And even if it was just pretend, even if it was just for these next two weeks, I was going to do my damnedest to show her that.

Platonically, of course.

* * *

The resort ballroom area was filled with what looked like all of Close-to-Custom's employees. I'd come down here while

Luna was still getting ready, knowing I needed to pick up our badges and sign us in before the welcome party.

Banners and signs lay strategically around the resort, the smooth matte design popping with bursts of hot pink and blazing gold around their company's logo. It was eye-catching, for sure. Their branding was one of the reasons why I'd researched their company in the first place.

It was sleek, clean, and had a wide appeal, plus the concept alone was brilliant—who didn't want their clothes to feel like they were custom made? Their app gave online shoppers the added benefit of being able to virtually try on items to see how they looked, but also ensure they got the perfect fit. The technology had already streamlined several online shopping venues, cutting their returns by thirty percent.

Those were solid numbers, and with some extra backing, the app could be developed further and integrated into more online stores—which was what this trip was all about.

I wanted to be that backer. I wanted to have a piece of this company for myself because I believed in their intentions. Beyond the evidence of it being profitable, the owners were renowned for being family oriented, inclusive, and forward-thinking. Pair that with the fact that they only allowed their app to be used by brands they believed in and matched their core values, and I was all for it.

Also, it was an easy sell for me because my best friend happened to be an incredible designer, so I'd been around the fashion industry longer than likely any of the other investors here putting in their bids for the company.

Music filtered out from the ballroom, the melody light and fresh. I checked my watch, hoping Luna was all right. She never took very long to get ready, but maybe she'd gotten nervous? Tonight would be the debut of our fake relationship, and after the kiss we'd shared, maybe she was having second thoughts?

A pit opened up in my stomach with the thought, and I knew it had more to do with Luna's nerves than with me losing time with the owners.

"I'm here!" Luna called out, and I spotted her hurrying across the hallway toward me.

Holy fucking shit.

I swallowed hard, my eyes trailing the length of her body. She wore a simple, elegant black gown that hung down to her ankles, the neck a deep V and with only two thin straps holding it all up. Her red hair was gathered on one side, a perfect wave rolling through the strands, and her lips were a bright crimson, all full and pouty. Fuck, she looked like Hollywood royalty from the twenties, all luscious curves and smoky hazel eyes.

"I know, I'm late," she said once she reached me. "I'm sorry. This wave thing is a lot harder to do than the girl on YouTube made it look." She motioned to her hair, flashing me an apologetic look.

"You nailed it," I said, finally finding my voice. "You look gorgeous."

A flush raked over her cheeks, her eyes quickly finding the floor. "Thanks," she said, almost too soft for me to hear.

Anger sliced right through the need barreling through me. Her ex had done way more damage than I'd even known about. She could barely take a compliment without trying to make herself smaller.

Asshole.

I stepped closer to her, offering her my arm. "You ready to have some fun?"

She brightened at that, slipping her arm through mine. "So ready."

I grinned down at her, guiding her through the opened double doors of the ballroom, instantly transporting us into the welcome party that was kicking off in full swing. Couples were already dancing, while some stood around high-top tables with drinks and food.

Pride made my chest puff out just a fraction as we walked around the room, so many eyes were on Luna with appreciative gazes. I fucking loved that she was on my arm. Loved that even if it was pretend, she was mine tonight.

"So, what's the official plan?" Luna whispered into my ear when I stopped at an empty table.

I grabbed two champagne flutes from a waiter passing by, and slid one to her. "Once I see an opening with the owners, we'll go over and introduce ourselves."

Luna nodded, taking a quick sip of champagne. "Oh," she said, her eyes flaring wide. "That's good." She took another drink.

I smiled at her, taking a drink myself.

"Is there anything I can do to help?" she asked. "Besides be..."

"My fiancé?" I finished for her.

"Right."

"Just be yourself," I said, but my chest warmed a bit knowing she wanted to help me seal this deal.

She didn't have to do this. Hell, she didn't even have to take an interest in it. I'd dragged her into this situation, and she could just as easily tune out and just enjoy the free vacation, but that wasn't Luna. She'd always cared about my interests, and it meant more to me than she knew.

"Myself," she said, almost like she was asking a question. "You want me to be myself?"

"Always," I said, furrowing my brow.

"Like my fashion-obsessed, dessert addict, romance novel devouring self?"

"Yes," I answered. "I'm not sure if you've noticed, but I'm pretty fond of you."

She held up her flute. "Okay," she said, clinking her glass against mine. "To being ourselves, only...*engaged*."

"That reminds me," I said after taking a sip of the drink. I sat it down on the table, reaching into my suit jacket pocket. "I meant to give this to you earlier." I took her left hand with my free one, and slid the ring onto her ring finger discreetly, not that anyone was paying attention to us.

"Omigod," Luna gasped, her features pure shock as she looked down at the ring.

It was a simple gold band with a square-cut emerald in the center, but from the way she looked at it, I could've just handed her the biggest diamond in the world.

"Brad," she said, her eyes fluttering from the ring to me and back again. "It's...it's..."

"Is it okay?" I asked, suddenly nervous I'd picked the wrong one. I mean, yeah, I knew this wasn't real, but that didn't mean she couldn't have something she actually liked to wear while we were playing pretend, right? "I know you've always liked emeralds more than diamonds, but if you hate it we can swap it—"

"It's perfect," she cut over me, and I swore there were tears in her eyes. But that couldn't be right. "I love it. It's exactly what I would've picked if..." She shook her head, a wide smile shaping her lips. "I might have a hard time giving it back at the end of all this."

I laughed, shaking my head. "That's yours to keep as long as you want it," I said. "Consider it one of many prizes I'll shower you with for doing me this solid."

She clapped, then threw her arms around me. I held her to me, inhaling her scent and relishing the way she fit so damn perfectly in my arms.

"This was the best idea ever," she said, pulling away.

And fuck me, her smile was infectious. The woman was

dazzling on every level, so much so I almost forgot why we were even here in the first place.

"Oh, isn't that the owners?" Luna asked, eying a table a few down from us.

"How did you know?" I asked, spotting them easily.

"I read all about them last week," she said. "And I might've stocked their TikTok accounts. They're really cool."

I beamed at her, surprised at the effort she'd put into this trip, even though I shouldn't be. Luna never did anything half-assed, perfectionist that she was.

"Let's go say hello," I said, guiding us over to their table now that they'd had a break in visitors.

"Mr. and Mrs. Ideson," I said, reaching out my hand as I approached their table. "Brad Washbrook."

Ezra Ideson smiled at me, recognition flashing in his eyes as he shook my hand. "Glad you were able to make it," he said, dropping my hand and sliding it around his wife's back. "This is my wife, Ava."

"Nice to meet you," Ava said, shaking my hand.

"This is my fiancé, Luna," I said, turning toward Luna, who smiled graciously and shook their hands as well. "We're so grateful for the invite. This is one hell of a welcome party."

Ezra grinned as he scooped up his drink. "Our employees deserve it," he said, motioning to the packed room with his drink. "They work extremely hard for us, so we wanted to give them a trip to remember, plus a much-needed break."

"Wow, can I come work for you?" Luna teased, and we all laughed.

"We're always hiring," Ava said. "Especially with the possibility of expansion soon." She eyed me, her dark eyebrows raised. "Which is why you're here."

"Absolutely," I said. "I'm a fan of your company and the message you put out in the world. I'm hoping after this trip, you'll consider me as a backer."

"Ahh," Ezra said, waiving me off. "No business tonight, Brad. It's a party. Have fun, enjoy yourselves. It's what we'll be doing." He tucked his wife closer to him, leaning down to steal a quick kiss. "There will be plenty of time for you and the other investor to give us your thoughts."

"Thank you," I said, nodding to them as someone called them across the room.

"That went well," Luna said. "Don't you think?"

"Definitely," I said. "I knew business wasn't going to happen tonight. It was good to put a face to the email chain though."

"Oh! There's a chocolate fountain!" Luna's hand flew to my forearm, her eyes focused on the space where all the food tables were stationed. "Can we?"

I furrowed my brow as I studied her. She was *actually* asking. Like I'd say no.

He probably did all the time.

Fuck that guy. If I did one thing right on this trip, it would be showing Luna how she deserved to be treated.

"You never have to ask," I said, heading with her toward the dessert station.

"I need to travel with you more often," she said, loading up a plate with strawberries before drenching them in chocolate.

"It's been a while," I said, getting my own plate before we headed back to our table. "What was the last trip we took?" I considered. "Greece?"

Luna nodded, her lips wrapping around the strawberry in a way that made my muscles tight. Fuck, those lips were dangerous, all plump and kissable. "That was almost six years ago," she said. "My parents got so drunk on that trip." She laughed.

"Mine too," I said, shaking my head. Our families had

been friends since before we were born, and we'd been taking trips together since we were kids.

But this trip was different. It wasn't a family thing, it was a me and Luna thing, and I couldn't help but revel in that.

"I haven't taken a real vacation since before I opened the shop," she said after a few more bites. "I didn't realize how much I needed this."

"Then we should do it more often," I said before I could stop myself. "Everyone deserves a vacation, and not just one every six years."

Luna smiled at me, chasing some stray chocolate from her lip with her tongue. I tracked the move, the need to span the distance between us and see just how much she tasted like chocolate almost bringing me to my knees.

"I know," she said. "But you know I have a hard time delegating. It's all I can do to let Janice run the shop when I have appointments. But she's definitely stepped up for this trip."

"She's been with you since the beginning," I said, referring to her single employee. "She'd never let you down."

"It has nothing to do with her," she said. "You know how I am."

"Perfectionist all the way," I said. "It's okay to let other people help you sometimes. That's what all the greats do."

She laughed at that. "I never said I was a great business person."

"But you are," I said. "Don't you see that? Luna, your shop is one of the best-selling boutiques in Sweet Water. Hell, people from Charleston drive down all the time just to buy your clothes. Imagine what would happen if you actually advertised your line?"

Her eyes flared with a combination of excitement and hesitation. "What if I do that and nothing sells? What if I spend all the resources to push it out on a wider scale and it fails?"

I shrugged. "What if it blows up? You're so focused on

what could go wrong, you aren't even considering what could go right."

"And you want to help me," she said.

"You know I do." I'd begged her to let me back her clothing line for years, ever since she started making repeat pieces for her store. "I know how your parents are with the control over your fund," I continued. We'd never seen eye-to-eye on the way they dictated Luna's spending, but she'd carved out a wealthy life for herself on her own. "I would love to help you in any way I can. Contacts, investment, whatever you need."

She stared up at me, her eyes a little wonderous looking, almost as if she was allowing herself to envision this dream for the first time.

"When you put it that way..." She took another sip of her drink. "I'm in."

"Seriously?"

"Yes," she said.

I scooped her into my arms, spinning her from the excitement coursing through me. She laughed when I set her on her feet.

"And if it fails—"

"It won't," I cut her off.

"If it fails," she continued without acknowledging me. "I'll pay you back. Somehow. I'll find a way. I owe you—"

"Nothing," I said, and grabbed two more champagne flutes from a passing waiter.

We clinked our glasses together, toasting to the new venture. This trip had already proven a success, and now all we had to do was enjoy it.

Three hours later, we settled back in our room. Luna came out of the bathroom in a pair of white cotton shorts and a purple T-shirt. Her hair was relaxed now, her makeup long gone.

Damn, the woman looked radiant even in her pajamas.

"Such a fun night," she said as she stopped at the foot of the bed. I was already on one side, leaning against the head-board while I'd finished responding to a few emails. "I'll be dreaming about those strawberries for weeks."

I grinned at her, setting my phone on the charger on the little table next to the bed.

"Speaking of dreaming," she said, pointing to the mattress. "One bed?"

"It's what they gave me when I checked in," I said. "I didn't realize until we got up here. I can sleep on the couch if you want." I motioned to the small sofa across the room.

She shook her head, rounding the bed and climbing in on her side. "I'm okay with it as long as you are," she said, sliding beneath the covers. "It's not like we haven't slept together before." Her eyes flared as the words caught up with her mind, and she laughed. "I mean, sleep...you know what I mean."

"I do, but it's cute when you get flustered, so keep going."

She playfully batted my chest, and I shifted to my side so I could face her. She mimicked my movement, tucking one arm beneath the pillow.

"Do you usually sleep in sweats and a T-shirt?" she asked, the question giving me a little whiplash.

"No," I admitted.

"You don't have to wear armor on my account," she teased. "I promise not to maul you in your sleep. I want you to be comfortable."

My lips parted open, but I just laughed and shook my head. "Okay then," I said, gathering my shirt with one hand and pulling it over my head. I shucked my sweats next, leaving me in what I normally slept in—my boxer briefs.

Luna's eyes widened, and her gaze turned deliberate as she took in my appearance, and when they lingered on my abs, I did a silent victory dance. I'd always tried to make time to stay active and in shape, but the look she gave me? Worth every single drop of daily sweat.

I shifted, turning off the light before laying to face her again. She was so close, with only a small space separating us. All I had to do was reach across the bed and pull her to me, slant my mouth over hers and claim it like I wanted to every other inch of her body. Tension twisted inside me, my body and heart warring with what it needed verses what it wanted.

"Good night, Brad," she said, closing her eyes.

I blew out a tight breath, digging up all the willpower in the world to lock down my emotions. "Good night, Luna."

Who was I kidding? This was going to be an impossible two weeks.

CHAPTER 7

Luna

Warmth surrounded me, lapping against my body like a calm island tide. I was in that wonderful space between sleeping and waking, my senses sluggish as they tried to pull me to the surface.

After a few seconds, I realized I wasn't on my pillow, but something warm, muscled, and moving up and down in a peaceful rhythm that was beyond relaxing. The smell of sage and mandarin swirled around me, making my heart flutter. I shifted against the warmth, noting my leg was hiked over something that my brain finally registered as *someone.*

Instinct had me drawing closer, my blood spiking with a shot of heat when I felt strong arms holding me tight. I'd never felt more safe or more exhilarated, my adrenaline rising as I tilted my head, desperately searching for a kiss I needed more than my next breath.

A powerful hand slid down my back, cupping my ass and squeezing. A thrill shot straight through the middle of me, the sensation waking up every aching portion of my body—

And my mind.

My eyes popped open, and I gasped, jolting at the very tangled state I was in with Brad.

Brad. My best friend. Not someone I'm supposed to be basically dry humping in the middle of the night!

Omigod, kill me now.

Brad's eyes opened as I jolted against him, and it took a few seconds before he realized our position. He released me, hands flying in the air like I'd been hot to the touch.

I scrambled off the bed, chest heaving and mortification washing all over me.

"I'm sorry!" I blurted, unable to *not* look at him lying in the bed, covers thrown off of him, his half-naked body on full display. Jesus, who looked like that? All carved muscles, tousled hair, and blue-gray eyes that were just this side of molten.

"It's okay," Brad said, his voice calm and reassuring when mine was borderline shaky.

"It's not okay, I was basically force-cuddling you!"

He laughed. The man actually *laughed*.

"This is so not funny!"

Brad smirked, a purely confident smile as he tucked one muscled arm behind his head, settling back against the pillows. "I mean, I am pretty awesome to cuddle with," he said. "It's not your fault you couldn't resist me."

I shook my head at him, rolling my eyes.

"I *can* resist you," I said, totally determined to make myself believe that. My sleep-induced-self had been ready to climb on top of him and kiss him until I couldn't see straight.

Was it going to be like that every night? Or was this just a fluke? God, maybe I should sleep on the sofa.

"Luna," Brad said, his supportive, sexy tone wrapping all around my name in a way I'd never noticed before.

Had he always said my name like that? Had I just not

noticed? Or was my body reacting to him in this way because of my horrific breakup? Shit, I needed to get a grip.

"I need to get ready for the breakfast," I said, not able to look at him lying there half-naked for one more second.

I grabbed my clothes for the day and my phone and speed-walked into the bathroom, shutting and locking the door behind me. I hurried to my group text, sending out an S.O.S.

Me: I just woke up with my legs wrapped around Brad.

Zoe: Holy shit.

Lyla: Brad, Brad?

Anne: That's so hot!

I laughed at their different responses, furiously typing on my phone. They all knew that this trip was a fake situation built to help Brad get more time with the owners of the company, so it was nice having a crew to talk to during my panic.

Me: I didn't mean for it to happen. But there's only one bed.

Lyla: One bed! Just like a romance novel.

Anne: Did you kiss him yet?

Zoe: Have you two discussed boundaries and terms?

Leave it to my psychologist best friend to ask about boundaries.

Me: We practiced a kiss once. And no boundaries.

Anne: How was it?

Lyla: Was it a good kiss?

Zoe: You kissed him and didn't tell me?!

Their messages came in at the same time, and I blew out a breath.

Me: It all happened so fast.

Lyla: And it's still a fake thing?

Anne: It doesn't sound fake.

Zoe: You need to set up boundaries.

Me: It is fake. For sure. This is all to help him. I just accidentally cuddled my best friend while asleep. It's not a big deal. Right?

I needed them to tell me it wasn't, needed them to help shake some sense into me. Because the last thing I needed right now was to be having feelings for one of my oldest friends, let alone *anyone*. I'd just had my heart broken by the only man I'd ever been with, which meant I was in no place for a relationship. Not that Brad even thought of me in that way.

But his kiss had felt so real—felt like the tipping point to a world of possibilities.

Anne: You never answered us about the kiss.

Of course, Anne would be the one to be direct and to the point. I loved that about her.

Lyla: I'm definitely curious.

Zoe: ...

My heart stuttered in my chest, an unstoppable smile shaping my lips.

Me: It was the best kiss of my life.

Zoe: !!!

Lyla: Awww.

Anne: You have to go in for more then.

Me: More? I can't. This is all a ruse.

Anne: You're both grown adults. If it feels that good, why stop there? Life is too short to skip out on good chemistry.

A thrill rushed through me as I read her text. Could I do that? Could I ask Brad to take this charade one step farther in the name of chemistry? Wouldn't that change the dynamics of our friendship? How would we ever be able to go back to being friends if we crossed that line?

Me: I don't want to lose him as a friend.

Lyla: That's a tough spot.

Zoe: I understand that.

Anne: You don't want to miss out on something awesome either. Trust me.

I knew Anne was likely referring to her relationship with Jim when it came to missing out. She'd spent the better part of a decade running away from her feelings for him, only to find out he was the best thing that ever happened to her.

"You good?" Brad called through the closed bathroom door.

"Yeah!" I hurried to answer. "Almost done."

Me: I have to get ready for a breakfast event. I'll keep you posted.

Zoe: You better!

Anne: Don't deny yourself anything fun!

Lyla: Tell me how the food is!

I laughed at my friends' responses, then set my phone down and hurried to get ready. Fifteen minutes later, I was fully dressed in a pair of loose white cotton pants and a simple T-shirt, my hair hanging down in waves over my shoulders.

Another ten and Brad and I were walking toward the banquet hall where the company's breakfast had been set up. He casually slid his hand into mine as we walked through the opened double doors, and dammit, my heart *flipped* as he interwove our fingers.

Why? Why was my body doing this to me?

I kept my face even, not showing a hint at my internal debate as we headed toward the owner's table which happened to have two open seats. Brad situated me into a chair, setting his hands on my shoulders for a moment.

"I'll go get your plate," he said, smiling at me before heading to the tables piled high with an amazing breakfast spread.

"That is so sweet," Ava said from where she sat across the table from me. "How long have you two been together?"

I swallowed hard. We hadn't prepped for this question.
Shit. Shit. Shit.

"Almost all my life," I said, deciding to answer honestly.

"How's that?" Ezra asked, sipping coffee from a white ceramic mug, his free hand wrapped around the back of his wife's chair.

He certainly was handsome, with rich brown eyes, a wide nose, and curly black hair that was cut close to his head. And his wife was absolutely stunning, with long ebony braids that hung over her shoulders, and a delicate mouth that was almost always shaped in a soft smile. The two looked like a power couple, all passion and love in their eyes.

"We've been friends since before I can remember," I said. "Our families are friends, so that's how we met. We've grown up together."

"I love that," Ava said, just as another couple returned to their seats next to Ava and Ezra.

"Love what?" Brad asked as he slid a plate in front of me.

The plate included pancakes, almost-burned bacon, fruit salad, and a little packet of Nutella to put on the pancakes—all of my favorites. My heart expanded in my chest, almost too big to breathe around. The urge to cry suddenly swept over me, but I sucked in a sharp breath, flashing Brad a grateful look as he sat down. Jesus, I was about to cry over the fact that he remembered my favorites, what was wrong with me?

You let Dennis ignore your needs for years all under the guise of being loyal and hopeful to help him change back into who you fell in love with in college.

Right. And he hadn't been that guy for years—the one who'd courted me, paid attention to me, acted like he loved me for me. And I'd lost sight of myself somewhere in between.

"That you two were friends before you fell in love," Ava answered him as he took his seat next to me, a plate of his own before him.

Brad glanced at me, a genuine smile on his face. "I would highly recommend it," he said. "Being with your best friend is definitely the way to go."

An excited little thrill rushed through me, despite knowing his words were all for show. I guess I couldn't be too mad at my body for responding that way, especially when it felt so damn good to be desired and treasured for once.

Dennis had never said anything like that to me before, and he certainly would never have fixed me a plate of all my favorite foods.

So, fuck it, even if it was fake, I was going to enjoy the hell out of this.

"Where did you say you met Marla, Craig?" Ava asked, looking at the couple on their right.

"I picked her up at a bar downtown," Craig said. He was about Brad's age and wore a three-piece suit, which looked a tad out of place where the rest of us were dressed casually. "Not all of us can have classic love stories," he continued before shoveling more food into his mouth. "But we do all right, don't we, babe?"

His wife, Marla, pursed her lips in a tight smile. "Yep." She nibbled on some fruit, looking like she'd rather be anywhere else.

"If you let my firm invest in your company," Craig continued, eyes on Ezra. "We'd be able to get your app into foreign markets. That's where the real profits are."

Ah, so this was the other investor vying for Ezra and Ava's attention. He definitely wasn't being subtle about it either.

Ezra shifted in his chair. "This is breakfast," he said, motioning to his food. "Not a business meeting."

Ava smiled at him, tucking into her food.

I did the same, doing my best not to moan at the flavors. Whoever catered the event was absolutely crushing it.

"What did they put in these pancakes?" I asked after taking another bite. "It's like fluffy heaven."

Ezra laughed, leaning forward. "Sweet cream."

"Really?"

"Her favorite." He motioned to his wife. "I asked the chef to prepare them that way."

Ava ran her hand over his back. "You're too good to me."

Ezra shrugged. "Never."

"I love it," I said, taking another bite. I'd have to tell Lyla about these and beg her to recreate them when we got back.

"Yes," Craig said a little aggressively. "It really is delicious."

"I'm more of a biscuit guy," Brad said.

Ezra laughed. "I hear you," he said. "Have you ever tried the Biscuit Company in Charleston?"

"Oh, they're the best," Brad said. "I usually take home a dozen even after eating a full meal there."

"Same," Ezra said.

"Biscuits are nice," Craig said, leaning forward to catch Ezra's eye.

I got secondhand embarrassment watching him force his way into every conversation just to get the owner's attention. I mean, yeah, I understood he was trying to land a deal, but come on. Who would respond to such fake aggression?

I knew Brad and I weren't technically engaged, but at least Brad was being a hundred percent real and himself in every other facet.

After an hour of more casual chitchat between us and more forced business comments from Craig, Ezra finally threw his hands up.

"Okay, okay," he said to Craig. "I get it. You want some serious time with us."

Craig's eyes lit up at that.

"I'm guessing you do too?" Ezra asked Brad, who looked more interested in his coffee than anything at that moment. It almost made me laugh. "Though you haven't been breathing down my neck about it."

I *did* laugh at that one.

"Of course, I do," Brad answered. "I just enjoy a business-free breakfast as much as the next person."

Ezra nodded, looking between Brad and Craig. "Okay, well I have a deal for you. The company is going to participate in a city scavenger hunt today. If one of my employees wins, then they'll get the custom prize of an all-expenses paid vacation. But, if one of *you* win, I'll raffle off that vacation so one of my employees still gets it, and your prize will be an hour of uninterrupted time with us to give us your full pitch, a whole week sooner than our already scheduled time that I made when I invited you both here." He eyed Craig. "I wanted you here for the retreat to learn about my company before you make your pitch, but it seems like some of you feel like you already know what you need to."

"Oh, hell yes!" Craig said. "You're going down, Washbrook!" He jabbed a finger toward Brad, using a tone that sounded like he was about twelve years old.

Wow.

Well, I wasn't going to let him get away with that.

"What are the rules?" I asked.

"I'll text you everything," he said, and I slid my phone across the table so we could exchange numbers.

Once he texted the requirements—which were extensive and looked like *so* much fun—I hurried to pocket my phone, pushing away from the table and reaching for Brad.

"What are we doing?" he asked, taking my hand.

"We're going to go win you that hour," I said, then winked at Ezra before we hurried out of the banquet hall.

"Shit!" Craig grumbled behind us, and I laughed as I heard him struggling to get Marla away from her coffee.

"Come on!" I urged Brad when he was dragging his feet.

He laughed, upping his pace as he followed me out of the resort. "What's the rush?"

"There are thirteen items on this list and they're probably

scattered all over the city. We only have until five to find them and text pictures to Ezra as proof. There is no way in hell I'm letting Craig win."

"I love it when you get competitive," he said as I hailed a cab.

I grinned at him, holding open the cab door for him and waving him in. "Let's go win you that hour."

* * *

Snap a selfie with the goddess of the sea and you'll be done with trying to win me.

I read the final clue on the company scavenger hunt as we stood outside the last landmark the hunt had taken us to. The little bar was a local favorite and had been established over fifty years ago. Brad and I had already snagged the photo we'd needed of a little gold English bulldog emblem situated on the wall next to an obscure booth inside.

We'd spent all day hunting down Ezra's items, using the clues he texted hourly as we navigated our way around the city. I had to hand it to him, he had chosen some pretty awesome landmarks, not to mention given some hilarious yet difficult clues to find them. We'd run into several groups of his employees who were working together for the prize, and they were all having a ball playing the company's game.

And while Brad and I were having a blast, I was determined as hell to win. Brad deserved that one-on-one time with Ezra and Ava, and if there was a way I could help? I was all in.

We'd been the first ones at the bar, and spotted a few more groups finally heading this way as we contemplated the final clue.

"We're ahead," I said, chewing on my bottom lip. Adrenaline surged through my veins, the need to go-go-go pulsing through me like a beating drum.

"Only because you've been rushing us around the city," Brad said, playfully bumping my shoulder with his. "I think the point of the hunt was mainly to enjoy every landmark Ezra sent us to."

"Maybe for his employees," I said, swiping on my phone to pull up a search browser. "But not for the investors pitching him." We'd only seen Craig once as we were leaving a spot a few hours ago. I hated the idea of him somehow gaining an advantage on us and beating Brad out of his time.

I typed in *goddess of the sea* in the search bar and squealed when an image popped up. "Got it!" I was already hailing a cab before Brad had even blinked.

"I haven't seen you this determined since junior year in high school when Ms. Skyler assigned us the storefront final," he said as he climbed into the back of the cab with me.

"That was just as serious," I said, grinning as the cab weaved in and out of traffic. "I wanted that two-hundred-dollar gift card."

"And you won it," Brad said. "All those freshmen bought out your clothes in record time. You completely obliterated my cookie storefront, not to mention all the other competition."

A warmth spread through the center of my chest at the memory. The assignment was the first indication to me that I wanted my own boutique, and now here I was, all these years later with a shop of my own and a potential national clothing line on the way. I worked hard, but I knew how lucky I was too.

"I bought most of your cookies," I said as the cab pulled up to our location.

"You took pity on me."

I grinned at him before paying the cab driver and opening the door. "No way," I said as we climbed out and onto the sidewalk. "You know I'm a sucker for anything sweet."

"Me too," he said, eyes trailing the length of my body for a few seconds longer than necessary.

It made a warm shiver race down my spine, swirling up all kinds of aches in my core. The kiss replayed in my mind, making my eyes fall to his lips without my permission. Damn, they still looked pretty freaking kissable.

"Where are we headed?" he asked, a slight smirk on his face.

I cleared my throat and spun around, heading toward the beach.

"Over here," I explained as he followed me.

The ocean stretched out in a beautiful swatch of blue and green on the horizon, the little touristy area just before the beach lined with a decent amount of foot traffic. Salt tinted the air, and the sun was warm on our faces as we navigated the small crowds of shoppers until I spotted it.

"There!" I hurried over to the statue, stopping just before it.

"Nice," Brad said, nodding as he looked up at the mermaid and dolphins swirling together to create one gorgeous statue, especially with the sea as its backdrop.

I furrowed my brow as I walked around the structure, wondering just how I was going to get a selfie with the goddess of the sea—she was a great deal taller than me, after all. After a few circles, I found a good place to get a leg up, and managed to lift myself with my phone in one hand.

"I don't think he meant a literal selfie, Luna," Brad said, concern lining his features as he stepped just beneath me.

I glanced over my shoulder and down, smiling at him. "I don't want to take the chance that he *did* mean it literally and not get it. It'll only take a second."

Brad sighed. "I really don't think you're supposed to be up there—"

"I'm not touching the statue," I cut over him, climbing up

on the base of the structure and reaching up on my tiptoes. I got my face in line with the mermaid, put on my best selfie grin, and snapped the photo. I stepped down while simultaneously texting the evidence to Ezra, nothing but a victory tune ringing in my head.

I misstepped and slipped backward, my heart lodging itself in my throat as my spine aimed straight for the pavement—

A pair of strong arms braced my fall, and Brad hauled me up, one arm under my knees and the other cradling my back as he held me against his chest.

"See," he said, his breath a little ragged. "I told you, you shouldn't climb up there."

"You caught me," I said, feeling utterly shocked and swoony at the same time. Who the hell catches someone without being in a movie?

"Of course, I did," he said, still holding me. "I'd never let you fall."

His words were so matter of fact, so obvious and sincere that they shot right through the heart of me. Adrenaline and need and relief coiled in one jumble of emotions that had me shifting in his arms until my mouth met his.

His mouth was warm and strong against mine, his instant response to the kiss making electricity crackle in my veins. His hold on me tightened, his lips working over mine in a sweet kiss that had heat licking up my spine. I fisted his shirt, kissing him harder, my heart racing against my chest as desire flickered to life inside me.

I didn't want to stop. I wanted more—

Reality struck me suddenly, forcing me to draw back.

We weren't pretending.

Not here, where no one needed to believe we were engaged. This was just me and my best friend. Me, *making out* with my best friend because he saved me from cracking my head open.

"I just wanted to say thank you," I said, eyes wide and breathing heavy. "I'm sorry."

Brad slowly shifted me, allowing my body to slide down the length of his as he settled me on my feet. His eyes never left mine. "I'm not."

My heart climbed up my throat, a whole heap of uncertainty and unbridled need slamming into me from all different directions. He smoothed a hand down my arm, never once attempting to take a step back and put space between us.

This was bad.

This was so very bad.

I didn't want him to step away.

I didn't want him to stop touching me like I worthy of devotion.

I didn't want him to do anything but keep looking at me with those blue-gray eyes of his with that look I couldn't read but oh so badly wanted to.

"Brad—"

My phone buzzed, snapping me back to a reality where we were in public and on a very important mission. I looked down, my eyes lighting up when I read the text. I flipped my phone to show him.

"We won," I said.

His smile was the most delicious thing I'd ever seen—all confidence, pride, and just a hint of desire.

"Have I ever told you how magnificent you are?" he asked, sliding an arm casually around my shoulders as he navigated us toward the busy street to hail a cab.

"Never," I teased.

He told me all the time, but it was easier to fall back into our friendly banter than deal with the very real emotions I was having a hard time denying.

"Maybe I will someday."

CHAPTER 8

Brad

"Thank you for taking the time to meet with me," I said, sitting across the table from Ezra. The place he'd picked for lunch was away from the resort where the retreat was being held, a little understated restaurant off of the tourist path.

"You earned it," Ezra said, taking a sip of his drink before the waiter came to snag our orders.

Luna had earned this lunch for me more than I did. I'd helped during the scavenger hunt, but she was the one who drove us toward the finish line.

A spike of need jolted my veins at the memory of her kiss after I'd caught her when she'd slipped from the statue. Fuck me, I couldn't stop thinking about it. It hadn't been pretend, hadn't been practice, it'd been spontaneous and *real*.

Sure, she said she'd only been thanking me from saving her neck, but still. I couldn't help but wonder if she wanted me as badly as I wanted her. Which was fucking unfair of me, since she'd just gotten out of a long and clearly emotionally abusive relationship. I wish I would've known. Wish I could've seen the signs. But they'd been together all throughout college, and

I'd done my best not to interfere with her relationship when on the surface she seemed so happy.

"Tell me a little more about why you want to step in as an investor," Ezra said, drawing me right back to the present.

Shit, normally I was the one who led these meetings, not the other way around. Luna was crowding my mind in the best of ways.

"I've followed your company since its creation," I explained.

Ezra arched an eyebrow at me. "I didn't expect that," he said. "Are you being genuine? Or are you trying to butter me up?"

I shook my head, appreciating his bluntness. "I'm not one of those investors who will try to placate you with fairytales," I said. "Just cold hard facts. I don't *need* a percentage in your company. I'm sure you've done your research too. You know I'm not hurting for any financial growth."

"I may have read up on you."

I nodded. "Then you'll know I only invest in companies I believe in."

"Fair enough," Ezra said just as the waiter brought us our food. "Then tell me," he said, scooping up his sandwich. "What made you look at our company? Are you a big fan of fashion?"

I took a bite of my chicken before answering. "Luna is a phenomenal designer," I said. "She runs a successful boutique in Sweet Water. She sells vintage clothes she sources from all over the world, and other odds and ends, but she also has a small section of pieces she made herself. I've been encouraging her to go wide with her own clothing line for a couple of years now, so I've done my research on online clothing sales and all the issues that go with it."

Ezra nodded, understanding flashing in his eyes. "You saw the same issue we did," he said.

"Yes." I took another bite. "The online clothing industry is a great way to reach a wider customer base, but the return percentages due to the wrong fit are astronomical. Your app changed that on the small scale, and I believe with more funding, it could change it on a much wider scale."

"So it's not just about the money for you," Ezra said.

"Not at all. I'm a businessman and I like profits, but I don't need them. I go for companies I know will succeed, and yours means more to me on a personal level because of my friend—connection with Luna."

Shit. That was close. I almost said *friendship* with Luna.

Guilt stabbed my insides. I'd just told the guy I wasn't an investor who would placate him to get his business, and here I was lying about having a fiancé just so I could get more time with him. But I wasn't lying about anything in regard to the business side of things, so that had to count for something.

"I respect that," Ezra said. "And Ava will too, when I relay this meeting to her."

"I'm guessing she wasn't up for a business meeting today?"

"She's running a panel for our team right now and going over our hopes for expansion or she would've been. We don't make big decisions like this without each other."

"I understand that," I said, knowing full well he wasn't about to draw up a contract for me right this second.

"And you know I can't give you an official answer until I've heard all the pitches," he continued.

I nodded, knowing Craig would likely have one hell of a pitch for him too.

"Understood."

"Then hit me with your numbers and your vision," Ezra said, waving at me to lay it on him.

So I did.

I gave him the full scope of my vision for his app

and how to perfect it, upgrade it, and give it a wider spread to more retailers across the country. I couldn't hide the passion in my voice either, didn't even try to. An app that used AI technology to scan a customer's body in real time to give them the best and most accurate fit of clothing was revolutionary for the fashion industry.

And it could do wonders for Luna's business if she decided to go wide with her line. She'd shown me her plan on the plane ride here, and it was almost ready to launch. She'd been working on it for far longer than I knew, but her asshole ex had made sure he buried that dream for her. Fucker didn't want her to shine as bright as she could.

"I have to say..." Ezra said after I'd finished my pitch. "I admire your passion. It's clear how much you care about the industry, and I suppose we have your charming fiancé to thank for that."

I swallowed hard. I was getting used to hearing Luna with that title, and I didn't hate it. Not even a little bit.

A pit opened up in the bottom of my stomach as I thought about the ticking clock above my head. I had less than two weeks to keep pretending she was mine before we'd go back home and just be friends again.

I didn't realize how much I hated that idea until now.

"When is the wedding?" Ezra asked, drawing me back to the table.

"We haven't set a date yet," I said, the lie rolling off my tongue a little too smoothly. But it felt like truth in my soul... we hadn't set a date yet because we weren't actually engaged, *yet*.

Fuck. A couple of kisses and I was ready to make that ring on her finger a reality.

Who was I kidding? I'd dreamed of a life with Luna long before we kissed, long before we played pretend. I'd never been able to act on it though, not while she was with her douchebag ex. And now...now things were complicated.

"That's not a bad thing," Ezra said, likely reading the distress all over my face. "Taking your time to figure out the right wedding and timing for you is the key to a great event."

I smiled, shoving all the complicated emotions down. "I believe you," I said. "You and Ava seem very happy."

"We are," he said. "She's the best thing that ever happened to me. I don't deserve her, but I try to every single day."

I smiled at him. "To the women who make us better men," I said, clinking my glass against his.

We shifted to small talk as we finished our lunch, and he let me pay after a quick check battle.

"See you at karaoke tonight?" he asked after we'd made it back to the resort.

"We'll be there," I said before he headed one direction and me the other.

And as I walked toward my and Luna's room, I couldn't stop the swell of pride in my chest at the thought of *we* and how damn good it felt to be paired with her in that way.

But it wasn't real.

And the more I thought about that fact, the more I realized how truly fucked I was.

* * *

"Are you sure you don't want to hop up there?" I asked Luna, motioning to Ezra and Ava who were currently crushing a song on the karaoke stage.

They'd converted the ballroom into a believable nightclub, and constructed a stage fit for even the most skilled karaoke aficionados. The space was coated in muted blue lights and the staff was weaving through all the crowded tables with snacks and drinks.

"Hell no," Luna said, laughing before she took a sip of her drink.

"Oh come on," I said. "We could do a duet."

She shook her head. "You know I'll listen to you sing all night," she said. "But I'm not about to subject these lovely people to my voice."

"I love your voice," I said, which only made her laugh harder.

"You're way too nice to me," she fired back, clapping as Ezra and Ava finished their song and a new singer took the mic.

"I feel like I'm the appropriate level of nice," I said.

"More than I'm used to," she grumbled under her breath.

"I hate that," I said before I could stop myself.

She arched a brow at me, but her eyes were soft, sad almost.

"It shouldn't be that way, Luna," I answered her silent question. "He should've treated you like a queen."

Luna laughed nervously. "I don't know about that—"

"I do," I cut her off.

"I don't need to be spoiled," she said. "I just..." She shook her head. "It doesn't matter anymore."

"It matters," I said, shifting so I was turned toward her and away from the stage. "What you want matters. What you *need* matters."

"He told me for years that I asked for too much," she said. "Hell, he's *still* telling me that."

"What?"

"He's been texting non-stop," she said.

"You're fucking joking."

"I wish I was," she said, reaching into her pocket before handing me her phone. "See for yourself."

I swiped open her phone, heading to her text messages. There were quite a few from Zoe, Lyla, and Anne, but I didn't dare read any of those and headed straight for Dennis's.

Dennis: You're being unreasonable. You at least owe me a response.

Dennis: The shit you're pulling is childish. I always told you how immature you could be. This is taking it to another level.

Dennis: I told you I was sorry. I want to make this work. I'll do better. I will.

Jesus, the texts went on forever. They started right after the breakup and kept coming in every day.

"Holy shit," I said as three dots appeared in the text.

"What?" she asked, leaning over my shoulder to look at her phone. She reached for it when she spotted the bubble, her eyes wary.

Then she *flinched*.

My girl actually flinched.

Not my anything.

She clenched her eyes shut, and I took the phone from her. She didn't stop me, so I figured I was good to go ahead and keep reading.

Dennis: You think someone else is going to put up with your bullshit? Good luck finding a man who will do the stuff you asked for in bed. That's not marriage material behavior. You're better off sticking with me. I can keep all that in check.

Rage washed over me so fast I had to set down her phone before I chucked it across the room.

"He's a piece of shit," I said, my jaw clenching.

Luna nodded, but her eyes were lined with silver as she took another drink. Her shoulders drooped, almost like she was curling in on herself, and it physically *hurt* for me to see her like that.

"Luna," I said, my voice soft. Fuck, what could I say to make it better? What could I do?

"It's fine," she said, trying her best to hide the pain in her eyes. "It's nothing I haven't heard before."

"You should never hear anything like that," I said. "Ever. You don't deserve that."

She shrugged, as if to say *maybe I do*, and I hated that he'd gotten her to that point mentally. "Let's forget it," she said, waving me off. "I just want to enjoy this party. These people are so fun. I might ask them for a job." She tried to smile, but the light didn't reach her eyes.

Fuck Dennis.

Every instinct in my body roared to find a way to make her smile like she was before he texted, before he spouted off a line of bullshit that made the joy in her eyes dim. Made her question herself.

The singer on the stage wrapped up, and I hopped out of my chair, grabbing the offered mic before asking the DJ to put on Better Days by Dermot Kennedy.

The music filtered through the surround sound speakers, the lyrics rolling through on the projected screen, but I didn't need them.

The was Luna's favorite song, and I'd memorized every single word. She'd played it enough that it was easy.

I brought the mic to my lips, looking down at her from my spot on the stage, and I sang.

I ignored all the whistles and impressed cheers from the massive crowd watching me, and focused solely on Luna.

Her eyes were wide, her lips parted as her features shifted from hurt, to shocked, to absolutely overjoyed, which only made me sing harder, louder. I moved around the stage as the song progressed, working my way down it and to our table as it neared its end.

Luna's chest was rising and falling, and her smile was bright enough to light up the entire ballroom. I dropped to my knees before her, bringing us to eye-level where she sat as I crooned out the last words of the song.

Cheers erupted around us, the applause overwhelming as I caught my breath.

Luna clapped before leaping out of the chair and wrapping her arms around my neck. I caught her effortlessly, hauling her against me as I brought us to standing. She pulled back slightly, her lips finding mine.

I clung to her, taking her kiss and claiming it. I slanted my mouth over hers, falling helplessly into the kiss as she opened for me. It was the sweetest, sexiest invitation, and I ignored all the voices in my head telling me this wasn't real. Instead, I dove right the fuck in, sliding my tongue between her lips, relishing the gasp that came from the contact.

It didn't matter that we were in a very public and crowded room, I wanted to splay her out on the table and take my time worshiping her body right fucking now.

She drew away just enough to look at me. Her lips were swollen from my kiss, and her eyes...

Fuck me.

They were churning, begging me to do just what I wanted with her.

CHAPTER 9

Luna

"I'm sorry," I blurted the words, my heart racing from Brad's kiss.

Or the kiss I initiated.

But he certainly didn't seem to mind.

"You keep saying that," he said, looking down on me, his eyes flickering from mine to my mouth and back again. The next singer came up to us, and Brad handed off the mic without even looking at the person.

He'd sang my favorite song...for *me*.

To make me smile.

To make me laugh. How could he be that amazing? I mean, I always knew how awesome he was, that's why he was my best friend, but add everything that had happened in the last couple days between us and I was seeing him in an entirely new light.

Our bodies were flush and his arms were still around me. I had no urge to move, no desire to put distance between us. My heart thumped in my chest, chanting more, more, *more*.

"I mean it," I said. "It's just..." I hesitated, shaking my head and dropping my eyes.

Brad gently tilted my chin up, forcing me to look up at him. "It's just what?"

I blew out a breath. It's not like I'd ever hidden anything from Brad before, so why start now?

"I've never been kissed the way you kiss me," I admitted, my cheeks flushing. It was even more mortifying when I said it out loud.

"Never?"

I bit my lip and shook my head. "Never."

It wasn't a lie or an exaggeration either. Brad's kiss was electric and consuming, sending jolts of need throughout my entire body. It was a kiss I could lose myself in and one I could find myself in just as easily. It was a kiss I knew would never be matched or beat.

Brad smoothed his hand over my cheek, tucking back some stray stands that had fallen over my face. "What else have you missed out on?" he asked.

I swallowed hard. He'd read the text Dennis had sent moments before Brad had launched into my favorite song. He'd seen what he wrote about what I wanted in bed. Was that what Brad was asking me now? Did he want to know what I'd wanted?

"It's fine," I said.

"What's fine?"

"The things I've missed out on," I answered. "I get it. I'm cute. I'm quirky. I'm the artist nerd who will never be viewed as sexy. I'm not the woman men lose their minds for. Dennis told me all the time—"

Brad shifted, sliding his fingers between mine and tugging me through the crowds of people still enjoying the party.

"We don't have to go," I said, doing my best to keep up with his pace. "We don't need to unpack my past. Let's stay. You've barely spoken to Ezra and Ava all night!"

"This is more important," he said, barely glancing over his

shoulder as he hurried us out of the ballroom and into the elevator.

"Brad," I said, shaking my head. "It's fine. Really. I promise. I'm fine."

He visibly swallowed, then hustled me out of the elevator and into our room before he locked the door behind us.

"What are you doing?" I asked, my heart racing, anticipation flaring through my veins. Brad didn't look like he'd dragged me in here to talk about my past and eat ice cream. He looked...God, what *was* that look?

"If you'll let me," he said, his tone rough as he loosened his tie with one hand, taking a deliberate step toward me before tossing it on the little table by the bed. "I'm going to show you just how fucking wrong he was."

Heat flushed every inch of my body.

"How?" I breathed the question.

"I'll fuck away every single negative thought he put in your mind."

My lips parted open, a thrill rushing through me at his words. He was practically prowling the distance between us now, and I retreated, not out of fear, but out of the sheer need for him to keep talking like that.

My back hit the wall, and he stopped in front of me, leaning an arm on either side of my face. I had to tip my head back to meet his gaze, and it *did* things to my body. Those blue-gray eyes were molten and hungry and...damn, I'd never had anyone look at me the way Brad was looking at me now. It was like he wanted to devour me.

"You..." I couldn't find my voice. "You don't mean that," I said. "You don't want me like that."

He couldn't. We'd never crossed that line before, but we'd never kissed like we had before either.

"Luna," he growled my name, dropping a hand and grabbing mine. He tugged it down and between us, settling right over something very hard and very large. "Does that feel like I don't want you?"

I gasped at the contact, at the forbidden territory, at the fact that he was rock hard when we'd only shared a quick kiss.

Desire flooded my veins, a need aching in my core.

He released my hand, and took up the lean against the wall again, caging me in as he looked down at me.

I didn't pull away. My heart thrummed in my chest, adrenaline making my breath short. I felt like I was about to step out of a plane and free-fall.

"You want me?" I asked, squeezing him over his pants.

"Fuck," he groaned, stepping closer into my touch. "Yes."

I dragged my hand over his length again, my mouth going dry at how much of him there was. I tried to get my voice to work, to ask the question I needed to—was this part of role playing fun or something more?

It had to be part of the role playing we were doing. Just an added bonus of the game. And that was fair, that was fine. I trusted Brad more than I trusted anyone. And if crossing this line with him felt even a fraction as good as his kiss, I'd be an absolute idiot to pass on the experience.

It didn't have to mean anything. I could protect my heart, and he clearly wasn't worried about anything changing between us, so why should I?

A shot of pure delight burst inside me as I mentally settled myself.

"Do you want me?" Brad asked, leaning down so that his lips hovered an inch above mine.

God, he smelled so damn good, *felt* so damn good in my hand.

"I don't know," I said, my voice totally emboldened. I don't know where this confident, sexual woman was coming from, but I definitely liked her, wanted to be here. Wanted to be the woman Brad made me believe I was. "Why don't you tell me?"

Brad's eyes guttered, and he didn't waste two seconds before gliding his free hand down my side, over my hip, and to the band of my pants. He kept his eyes locked on mine as he teased my skin beneath the fabric before gently plunging inside them, his powerful hand moving over the lace I wore.

I gasped as he shifted the flimsy scrap to the side, gliding his fingers between my thighs.

"Fuck," he groaned, stroking me. "You're so wet for me. I've barely touched you."

My free hand flew to his bicep, clinging to it because I felt like I might fall over as he stroked me.

"Brad," I breathed his name, arching my head back as he teased my sensitive flesh.

"Damn," he said, shifting closer to graze his lips over mine at the same time he slid a finger inside my heat. "You're so responsive, baby," he said against my mouth. "You're ready to come for me already."

God, I *was*.

I was more than ready.

And that...that had never happened before. I'd never been this turned on, and he was right, he'd barely touched me before now—

He slipped another finger inside me, stretching me, filling me. I moaned into his mouth, capturing his lips with my own. He kissed me back, his tongue sweeping into my mouth in a fiery claiming that lit up my entire body as he pumped his fingers inside me.

Instinct had me rocking against him, and he rewarded me by grinding the heel of his palm against my pulsing clit.

"Brad," I moaned, tearing away from the kiss to catch my breath. Everything in me narrowed to the feel of his fingers as he pumped and curled them, as he put just the right amount of pressure from his palm against me. Nothing else existed outside of the need driving and building inside me. "Brad, Brad, *Brad*," I gasped as my pleasure built and scraped the inside of my skin, threatening to rip me apart in the best way.

He increased his pace as he kissed down my neck, his teeth grazing over the sensitive patch of skin beneath my ear.

My toes curled in my shoes, and I gripped his arm as he ground his palm against my clit, over and over again as he pumped inside me until—

I *shattered*.

Combusted.

Spiraled in a swirl of pleasure that shook my entire body as I came on his fingers.

I gasped, my body trembling as the aftershocks took me on a fun ride all their own.

Brad kissed his way back up my neck, across my jaw, and over my lips, lingering there as he slowed his fingers before gently pulling them away.

"You're so fucking beautiful," he said, bringing his fingers drenched with *me* to his lips. I think my heart stopped as he sucked those fingers into his mouth, drawing them out slowly in the sexiest move I'd ever seen. "And you taste delicious too."

A warm shiver shook my body, which was limp with pleasure.

His mouth crashed against mine, and I opened for him, whimpering at the taste of me on his tongue as he stole my breath. "You want more?" he asked between our kiss, his hand gliding down my thigh and hiking it around his hip.

I gasped at the move, the position putting him between my thighs.

"Or do you want to stop here?" he asked, kissing me again. "You say the word, and we'll be done."

That sounded like the worst idea in the history of forever.

"Don't stop," I breathed the words, feeling slightly buzzed even though we hadn't drunk any alcohol at the party.

This was all Brad, what he did to me.

It was the game we were playing, the roles we'd fallen into. And I had no interest in going back to reality any time soon.

"If anything is too much," he said, his hands flying to the hem of my shirt. "Tell me to stop."

Anticipation burst in my veins, and I nodded as he lifted my shirt over my head and tossed it behind him. He tugged my pants down next, and I kicked off my heels before stepping out of them.

He took a step back, lips parted, eyes hazy as they trailed the length of my body.

I had the instinct to cover my stomach, something Dennis had always commented on. He never appreciated my curves and always left my shirt on whenever we did have sex. The memory almost had me curling in on myself as I stood there in just my lace bra and panties.

"You're the most gorgeous thing I've ever seen," Brad said, his tone scraped raw.

My lips parted open to argue, but I forgot how to speak when he started undoing the buttons of his shirt, sliding it off in a hurry before yanking off his pants.

Goddamn.

Brad was tall and lithe, his abdomen well defined. The black boxer briefs he wore did nothing to hide what I'd felt earlier—he was rock hard and *big.*

He stepped toward me again, his hands gliding over my body in an explorative way that I mimicked. I'd seen Brad in swimming trunks before dozens of times, but that was nothing compared to this. Nothing compared to having his hands on my body while mine were on his, touching and learning and craving.

Brad kissed my neck again before working his way down

and over my breasts that were threatening to spill right out of the lace. They more than filled his hands as he cupped them, teasing my nipples with the friction of the lace. I arched into his touch, my mind spinning with the sensation.

I'd never been touched like this—with such desire, such care. Dennis had never been into foreplay, never done anything to get me going before he plunged in and was done in a few pumps.

I reached between us, stroking Brad's length over his boxer briefs, my mind swimming with pleasure as he thrust against my touch.

"Fuck," he groaned, stepping just far enough out of my reach.

My stomach dropped, rejection flooding my system, my body remembering all the times I'd been told no or been scolded for attempting to try new things.

"You keep doing that and this will be over way sooner than I want," he said, dropping to his knees before me.

Every sense of rejection evaporated with the move, with the sight of him there. He smirked up at me, his fingers grabbing the hem of my lace. "And I want to keep playing," he said, dragging the lace down my legs until I had to step out of them.

I barely had time to register what he was doing before his mouth was between my thighs, his tongue spreading me.

"Brad," I gasped his name as he maneuvered me, keeping one hand on my hip as the other slid behind my knee and hiked it over his shoulder.

I gripped his shoulder with one hand and tangled my fingers in his hair with the other as he ate at me.

"Omigod," I moaned, arching into his mouth, my body reacting on instinct as I chased my pleasure.

"Mmm," he hummed before lapping at me, teasing my oversensitive clit.

I shivered, my breath ragged with each move, each thrust

of his tongue. I didn't know this kind of pleasure existed. I'd read about it in books a hundred times before, but I'd never experienced it before, and holy shit his *mouth.*

My entire body clenched, desire shooting to every nerve ending I possessed as he licked me. His powerful hand gripped my thigh resting over his shoulder, the quick bite of pain making me tremble as pleasure rippled along the edges of my body.

And then he looked up at me just as I was looking down at him, our eyes locking as he dragged his tongue up the center of me and I swear I melted into a puddle of desire and pleasure and bliss and ecstasy right then and there.

Then he smirked. The man *actually* smirked as he licked me. "I want you to come on my tongue, baby," he said against my sensitive flesh, right before he flattened his tongue against my throbbing clit, over and over again, using his leverage on my thigh to rock my body right into his face—

I threw my head back, digging my nails into his shoulder as my orgasm ripped through me, coming at me in crashing waves of pleasure that shook every inch of my body.

I barely caught my breath before Brad shifted off the floor, scooping me into his arms and carrying me to the bed. He gently laid me down, then stepped back to survey me.

"You want more?"

My body was weak with pleasure, but I was still achy and needy.

"Please," I practically begged.

He grinned, then took off his boxer briefs, his hard cock springing free.

"Wow," I said, unable to hold back the word.

"You like that?"

"Yes."

"You want me inside you?"

98

God, how the hell could he make me hot and needy with just his words?

"Yes," I answered.

He dug into his suitcase across the room, grabbing a foil packet and ripping it open before rolling a condom over his considerable length. Climbing onto the bed, he motioned to me.

"Lift that beautiful ass for me," he demanded.

It was amazing how quickly I obeyed.

He tucked a pillow beneath me, hoisting me up at a higher level as he positioned himself between my thighs. He smoothed his hand down my legs, leaning over to kiss my breasts, my neck, my lips.

I kissed him back, relishing the feel of his skin against mine as I ran my hands over every inch I could reach. I felt like I was one fire, slowly burning in the most beautifully delicious way, and I never wanted it to end.

"Are you sure?" he asked one more time, eyes locked on mine as he lined his cock up with my aching heat.

"Yes," I said. "*Please*. I've never needed anything so badly in my entire life."

That made his cocky smile deepen, and he didn't hesitate to inch his way inside me.

I gasped as he bottomed out, his cock filling and stretching me in a painfully pleasurable way. I wrapped my arms around him, then my legs as he held still, letting me adjust to his size.

Then I rolled my hips, urging him out of me before drawing him back in.

"Fucking hell, Luna," he groaned, pleasure rippling his features. "You feel so fucking good. All slick and hot." He pulled out and thrust inside me again, this time faster and harder.

"Brad," I moaned his name, my entire being centering around the way our bodies crashed together. The way our lips

99

met. The way his tongue felt gliding against mine while he pumped inside me.

"Is this what you wanted? What you asked for?" he asked, thrusting into me. "Or more?"

"This," I said, my mind spinning with pleasure. "And more," I continued."

"Show me."

There was no room for hesitation, for nerves, not when everything he did felt so damn good. I reached for his free hand, dragging it over my chest, positioning his hand over my throat.

"Goddamn," he groaned, taking over and giving my throat the perfect little squeeze.

I moaned at the sensation, at the dominance in the move. I'd read about it a dozen times in books, but never knew it would feel like this—pure submission edged with the sweetest pleasure.

"You're so fucking perfect." He kept his hand on my neck, pumping into me harder.

"I can't get enough of you," I breathed the words, raking my hands over his muscles. "You're..." I whimpered as he bottomed out, grinding against my clit while squeezing my throat just a fraction harder. "Amazing."

I tightened my thighs around his hips, holding him closer, urging him to go harder.

"Fuck, baby," he groaned, giving into my silent demands. He slammed into me, the angle from the pillow giving him all the access to go deeper, to stroke that spot inside me that had me seeing fucking stars. "I...*goddamn*, Luna."

"Yes," I moaned, meeting his every thrust, driving us both to that sweet edge of release. I lost myself entirely to sensation, letting my body direct what it needed, what it demanded from him. And he met each and every need and then some, pushing me to limits I didn't know I had and then crashing me right over them. "*Brad*."

I clenched around his cock, my orgasm intense and sparking as I came for the third time.

"Fuck," Brad groaned, following me right over that edge, rocking me right over the aftershocks and into a mind-blowing sense of bliss that settled over my entire body.

He braced himself with his arms on either side of me, leaning his forehead against mine as we caught our breath.

I was too tired to worry, to question what we'd just done, to ask out loud what it might change between us. Instead, a blissful little laugh bubbled right out of my lips.

Brad drew back, smiling down at me.

"What's so funny?" he asked.

I shook my head, reeling it in but I couldn't contain my smile. "I don't know," I said. "I'm just happy. Really, really happy."

He wet his lips, his eyes flashing serious for a second before he blinked it away, replacing it with pure mischief. "Good," he said. "That's all I ever want."

CHAPTER 10

Brad

"I have to confess something," I said to Luna as we headed toward the spa in the resort. It'd been two days since we'd crossed that line, since I'd had the best night of my entire life, and neither one of us had spoken about it or tried to cross it again.

"What's up?" Luna asked, her eyes flaring just a bit wider as she looked up at me where we stopped outside the spa.

I wanted to tell her I couldn't stop thinking about that night. Couldn't stop thinking about how perfectly we'd fit together, how the chemistry between us had been like nothing I'd ever felt before. How I loved that these last two days had been normal between us—nothing awkward or lingering—just pure fun while we continued to get to know Ezra and Ava and more about their company.

"I..." Fear strangled my voice. What if I told her I wanted more and she shut me down? What if she said it was a fun one-time thing that got me out of her system? Could I survive that? "I saw your website this morning while you were designing it."

Luna laughed, the sound somehow relieved. What had she

thought I was going to say? "You were looking over my shoulder?"

I held up my thumb and forefinger, only leaving a tiny space between the two. "Just a little. I loved it. It's got your voice all over the designs."

She pressed her lips together to try and hide her smile. It was adorable as hell, and pride swelled in my chest that I'd been the one to put that smile there.

Fuck, I'd made her skin flush and her eyes roll back in her head two nights ago, and it was one of the most incredible things I'd ever seen. I locked my thoughts down before I walked into the spa with my cock on full display.

"Thank you," she finally said. "I'm almost finished with the last of my designs. If I keep up this pace, I should be able to launch the site before we even finish this trip."

"That's incredible," I said, holding the door open for her and motioning her into the spa lobby. "I can't wait to see what happens."

She'd been busting her ass during the times we weren't attending parties, events, or lectures here at the retreat, and I admired the hell out of her for it. It was like now that she'd been freed of the shackles her ex had kept her in, there was no stopping her.

Luna shrugged, doubt flickering over her features. "Well, if it fails, I'll still have the boutique."

"Hey," I said, turning to stand in front of her. Fuck, she was gorgeous dressed in a pair of loose cotton pants and a simple T-shirt, her long red hair flowing over her shoulders in causal waves. "One, it won't fail. Two, you have to visualize your success. Spend your energy focusing on the *best* possible outcomes, not the worst."

Her eyes trailed up to mine, jumping between me and my lips and back again. Whatever she was visualizing had nothing to do with her clothing line, I could tell that by the way she worried her lip between her teeth.

I wanted to suck that lip into my mouth and hear her whimper again.

Jesus, it was all I could do to not reach between us and haul her against me, slant my mouth over hers and make her come right here in the damn lobby.

"Washbrook?" The receptionist called my last name, snapping both me and Luna to attention.

"That's us," I said, turning around to face the front desk, one arm effortlessly sliding around Luna's lower back and tucking her into my side. The motion was pure instinct, and the fact that there was zero hesitation as she leaned into me and placed her hand on my chest made me feel like I was walking on air.

"We're ready for you," the receptionist said. "Follow me please."

We followed her through a glass door and down another hallway before she motioned us into a room with two massage tables, the lights dimmed to a soft, soothing level. "Your therapists will be in shortly," she said before instructing us to disrobe into whatever level of comfort we liked before closing the door behind her.

"Wow," Luna said, surveying the luxury of the room. "I've never done this before," she admitted.

"Had a massage or a couple's massage?" I asked, furrowing my brow.

"Couple's massage," she said, then eyed the two massage beds. "I guess we should get undressed?"

She looked almost nervous as she said it, and I wondered how she could be self-conscious around me when I'd had my cock buried between her thighs and my fingers squeezing her perfect throat not two nights ago. And goddamn, that's what that asshole had said was unreasonable to ask for in bed? A little choking? I hated him even more, if that was possible, for making her feel bad about expressing what she wanted only because he didn't have the fucking chops to deliver.

"I'll turn around," I said after she continued to look a little nervous, and moved to do just that.

"It's okay," she said, stopping me. "It's not like you haven't seen it before."

We both laughed at that. Okay, so here was the little bit of awkward I'd expected to happen the morning after.

But that all vanished when she reached for the hem of her shirt and pulled it over her head, replacing the sensation with pure fire.

Fuck me. She moved to her pants next, standing there in nothing but a matching black set of lace that barely held her perfect breasts.

And I was hard.

Shit. That was not something I needed to be when the therapist came in, but at least I knew they'd knock first. I had time to get myself in check. I was a grown man for fuck's sake.

Luna wet her lips, reaching behind her to unclasp her bra.

Everything in me went tight as I watched her free herself of the restraint, her nipples peaked from the chill in the room. She gathered her clothes and put them on a little chair in the corner, then climbed on the nearest bed.

"Are you going to get a massage fully clothed?" she asked as she situated herself under the sheet on the massage table.

"No," I said, clearing my throat. "Can you blame me for being a little distracted?"

She bit that bottom lip again, something sad flashing across her eyes. "You don't have to say things like that," she said.

I hurried out of my clothes, leaving my boxer briefs on like she had her panties, and climbed under the sheet on the bed next to hers. "What do you mean?"

"I know you're just being nice," she said, nothing but pure doubt in her voice. "And it's super sweet of you, but like I said the other night…I know I'm not the typical model body type. I love food and I'm soft in all the places you're hard. It's fine."

I furrowed my brow, anger forcing my hands into fists. "That fucking asshole," I grumbled out loud. "Luna, you have no idea how damn gorgeous you are."

She visibly swallowed. "Brad—"

"No," I cut her off. "This is one instance where you don't get to argue with me. You know me. I would never lie to you. I'm not saying any of this to be *sweet* to you or because I'm your best friend. I'm saying it because I fucking mean it."

She turned her head so she could lock eyes with me, scanning my face like she was indeed searching for the lie, for the evidence that I was sugarcoating things to keep her happy.

That fucking guy did a number on her and I wanted to kick his teeth in for it.

"If that's true then why haven't you tried—"

A knock on the door cut over her words.

"Just a minute," I calmly called.

"Haven't tried what?" I asked, my heart thudding in my chest.

"Nothing," she said. "It doesn't matter."

"It does matter," I countered. "Tell me."

She wet her lips, hesitation shaping her features. "Why haven't you tried to…you know…" She struggled with her words, a flush raking over her skin.

I cocked an eyebrow at her, barely able to contain my smirk. "Tried to make you come again?"

She clenched her eyes shut. "Forget I said anything."

I chuckled, pure joy spearing through my veins. She wanted me to try? Fuck, all she had to do was say so. "Luna," I said. "Luna, look at me."

She pried open her eyes, looking at me with equal parts curiosity and mortification.

"You've practically hugged the edge of the bed these past two nights, putting as much distance between us as possible," I said. "I kind of took that as a cue to not cross that line again, but if that's what you want, all you have to do is ask."

"Really?" she asked. "I thought you didn't want to because you didn't act like it."

"I'm taking my cues from you, babe. I'll never push you into something you don't want."

A battle raged in her eyes, causing the cutest little crinkle in her nose.

"Do you want me to try?" I finally asked when she hadn't said anything. I swallowed hard, adrenaline coursing through my veins as I waited for her response.

"Yes," she said, then turned away from me, putting her face in the opening at the head of the massage table. "We're ready!" she called.

She wanted me to *try*.

She wanted me to court her, seduce her. And yeah, it was probably because we'd already fallen so deep into this game we were playing where she was my supposed fiancé, but I'd take what I could get.

The two massage therapists came inside, one going to either of our tables and giving us calm instructions before they started to work on us. It was hard as fuck to not look over at Luna every time a little sigh came from her lips as the therapist worked her tense muscles.

After.

There would be time after.

Because game or no, she'd given me the green light, and now she had no clue what she was in for.

* * *

"That was legit the best thing ever," Luna said as I held the door open for her to our room.

Her hair was a mess from the massage, but her eyes were that relaxed kind of glossy that happened when you'd had your muscles worked on by a professional.

"The best?" I teased, locking the door behind us. I really couldn't argue with her, the therapists had been top-notch. My body was free of knots and totally loose.

Her eyes met mine, then she shrugged. "Okay, maybe not the best *best*, but still, so good." She headed to the little fridge in the room and grabbed a bottle of water, tossing me one too.

I caught it, and we stood there in silence while we took hefty drinks as per the massage therapists' instructions. A few stray drops lingered on the corner of her lip, and I watched as she darted her tongue out to catch them.

Fuck, I wanted that tongue in my mouth again. Wanted to kiss every inch of her body again.

"I need a shower," she said. "I'm covered in lotion and oil from the massage." She tossed her empty water bottle in the recycling bin.

"Me too." I cocked a brow at her, crossing the room to toss my bottle in the bin, then offered her my hand.

She sputtered for a second. "You want to take a shower with me?"

Damn, as cute as it was for her to be constantly shocked at how much I wanted her, it made me just as pissed that she'd been beat down to be so doubtful about herself.

"Of course I do," I said matter-of-factly.

After a few seconds, she slid her hand into mine, and I led her through our room to the spacious shower in the connected bathroom.

I turned on the hot water, then turned to her, reaching for the hem of her shirt. I gauged her reaction, noting the hesitance there.

"We don't have to do this," I said. "If you don't want to—"

"I do," she cut me off. "I really, really do."

"But?" I asked.

"I've just...I've never experienced anything like this before. I don't know how to act, what to do. I don't want to do anything wrong. I know you've had way more experience than me in this department, so it probably isn't a big deal to you, but I'm terribly behind when it comes to this. Not because I didn't try..." Her voice trailed off, and she shook her head. "I'm totally ruining the moment."

I tipped her chin up to meet my eyes. "You could never do anything wrong," I said. "Not with me. And you're not ruining anything." My heart ached in my chest for how badly she'd been treated and how clearly I'd been oblivious to it.

I knew Dennis had been a dick, but I never thought he'd been making her feel like shit for wanting things sexually. Hell, she could ask me to wear nothing but an apron and fuck her in the kitchen while dinner was on the stove and I'd be into it.

"From here on out, Luna," I continued. "You don't need to doubt anything. Not with me. You tell me what you want, what you've been missing, and I'll do my best to make it happen."

"Because I'm your fiancé," she said timidly.

"For the next ten days," I said, hating that my gut twisted with the deadline. Hated that I couldn't tell if that's all this was to her or if I was simply a rebound after a really shitty relationship.

But I didn't care.

I'd take whatever pieces she gave to me.

I'd be whatever she needed, as long as it was *me* that she used for that need.

"Okay then," she said, pure delight lighting up her eyes as she stepped toward me, and tugged my shirt over my head.

I did the same for her, and soon we were bare as we stepped into the warm shower.

I navigated her under the stream of hot water, relishing the way she arched against the heat. I watched the drops cascade over her body, watched her nipples peak against the sensation, and groaned.

"You're so fucking sexy," I said as she dipped her hair beneath the stream.

She eyed me, trailing all the way down to my very hard dick. "You are," she said, running her fingers through her hair.

I grabbed the body wash, dumping a good amount into my hands before lathering up and stepping into her space. I ran my hands over her body, taking my time soaping her up. She did the same for me, our motions slow and deliberate like we had all the time in the world.

Ten days.

I only had her like this for ten more days.

I couldn't waste a second of it.

"Tell me," I said after we'd rinsed off. "Tell me what you want that you haven't gotten." I trailed my hands over her wet body, lightly teasing her nipples.

She sighed, arching into my touch. "It was just things like this," she said. "Attention, foreplay. I barely ever..." She didn't finish her sentence, and I shook my head as I gripped her hips and turned her so her back kissed my chest, the water spraying us down one side so it wasn't in her face.

"He didn't take care of you," I said, knowing that's what she meant. What a selfish fucking asshole.

"No," she admitted, her breathing ratcheting up the more I ran my hands over her body.

I leaned down, kissing her neck before grazing my teeth over that spot beneath her ear she loved so much. She arched from the sensation, causing her luscious ass to grind against my cock.

"He made you feel guilty for wanting things that made you feel good, feel excited." I dragged my hand over her breasts and down, gliding over her stomach before I found that sweet patch of curls between her thighs.

"Yes," she said, gasping as I slid my fingers through her heat.

Fuck, she was so wet and hot, like fiery silk. I stroked her with a light pressure, working her up in slow passes.

"Do you trust me to make you feel good, baby?" I asked, sliding a finger inside her. "Do you trust me to take care of you?"

"Yes," she breathed the word.

"Then put your palms against the wall and don't move them until I tell you to," I said, adding just a hint of demand in my tone. After she showed me the desire for my hand around her throat, I was more than ready to play the dominant role for her.

She did as she was told, and god*damn*, a rush of wetness met my fingers at the command. My girl liked to be told what to do, liked to be taken care of.

"Good girl," I said, adding another finger as I pumped them inside her.

I nudged her legs a bit wider with my knee, making room for me to bring my body flush against hers as I stroked her.

"*Brad*," she sighed my name as I stepped behind her, teasing my hard cock against the seam of her ass.

I ran my free hand down her spine before gripping a handful of that luscious ass and yanking her back against me. The wetness from the shower made us both slick, and my cock glided against her effortlessly, teasing her in places I assumed she'd never been teased before—that bastard always making her feel guilty for asking for the most basic things. Affection and attention and pleasure.

Fuck him. I'd make sure she got everything she wanted and

then some. I'd make sure she never questioned her pleasure and what turned her on ever again.

"You like that don't you, baby?" I asked, gliding my cock back and forth between her cheeks as I pumped my fingers inside her. "You like feeling me from all angles."

"God, yes," she said, her fingers curling against the shower wall.

Her breathy answers were fire in my veins. My cock ached with every tease, begging to sink into her heat and pound us both into oblivion.

I upped my pace, flattening the heal of my palm against her clit, giving her the pressure she needed to fly apart.

"Brad!" she gasped, rocking against my hand with unabashed need.

Fuck, it was hot as hell watching her ride my hand, each time she moved making her rock against my cock.

She clenched around my fingers, her orgasm making her thighs tremble as she shivered through the intensity of it.

I didn't waste a second before I pulled my fingers away and spread her even wider, dipping the tip of my cock in her wetness before pulling away again. Goddamn, she felt like a dream, all searing and pulsing for me. For pure torture's sake, I dragged myself through her again, making us both groan.

I kissed her shoulder, nipping lightly at her neck.

She arched back, rocking against me and almost managing to get my cock inside her before I pulled out of reach.

"Condom," I ground out the word. "Baby, I have to go get a condom."

"No," she almost whined. "Please. Don't go. I'm covered. And I'm clean. I was tested right after I found out Dennis cheated on me."

"I am too," I said, my mind whirling with the idea of sinking into her with nothing between us. "But are you sure?"

"God, yes, please, Brad." She pushed back against me,

using her leverage on the wall to wiggle until I was right where she wanted me.

And fuck me did it make me want to drop to my knees and worship her.

"Tell me you want me to fuck you," I demanded, my hands flying to her hips, holding her there on the edge. My cock poised right at where she pulsed for me.

"Fuck me," she said, breathless. "Now."

I slid in an inch, my muscles locking at the effort it took not to plunge right in.

"Like this?" I asked, drawing out the anticipation as I slid in another inch.

"God," she moaned, her only answer. She tried to push back, tried to take me all the way in, but I held onto her hips, keeping her there.

I brought my lips to her ear, nipping it lightly. "You feel so fucking good, baby," I whispered, sinking in another inch. "I can feel you pulsing around my cock."

She trembled, releasing a breath. "Brad," she said. "*Please.*"

"Please what?" I teased, kissing down her neck as I held us there.

"Please make me come again," she breathed the words, and I lost the control I'd held the whole time.

I slammed home, bottoming out inside her before pulling all the way out and doing it all over again. Each time she pushed back against me, meeting me thrust for thrust, syncing up in a rhythm that drove us both wild with need.

I gripped her hips, taking full control, moving her back and forth as I pumped my cock inside her, feeling every glorious inch of her heat without any barrier between us.

Luna was heaven, pure fucking heaven.

I stepped back, yanking her with me until she bent slightly against the shower wall. She whimpered at the new position, her pussy clamping around my dick in the best fucking way.

And then she let one hand fall from the wall, reaching behind to try and grab my hand.

I lightly spanked her ass, and she moaned from the contact, a flood of warmth slicking my cock as I thrust inside her. "What did I say about that wall?"

Her hand flew back to the wall, and I pulled my cock out of her, gliding it through her wetness and teasing it against her clit until she writhed against me, desperate for release. The warm water was starting to turn cool as it splashed against our skin, only adding to the sensations as I plunged back inside her again.

I pumped into her heat, my release coiling at the base of my spine, but I managed to hold it at bay. No way was I coming without her—

She took her hand away from the wall again, reaching behind to grip my bicep.

I lightly smacked her ass again.

"God, yes," she moaned, and I swear I saw fucking stars.

"Oh, so you want to be my bad girl, do you?" I teased, pumping into her in a hard, punishing way. "Is that it?"

"Yes, yes, yes," she said, the sounds of our sex filling the shower with how hard we were going now.

I tangled my hand in her hair, fisting it until she had to stand up a bit straighter, her back pressing against my chest as I continued to fuck her. She reached up, wrapping her arms around my neck, giving me a full view of her glorious body as she tilted her head up and back to meet my eyes.

Fuck.

I was such a goner for her.

One look.

She owned me with *one* fucking look.

I slanted my mouth over hers, releasing her hair and plunging my hand between her thighs, rolling my fingers over her clit while I thrust into her.

She moaned into my mouth, her pussy rippling around my cock as she came, her orgasm tearing through her and yanking mine out too. I spilled inside her, our bodies convulsing in sync as we crashed over the edge together.

I slipped out of her, spinning her in my arms as I gently cleaned us both up, then shut off the water and wrapped her in a towel as we stepped out.

She shivered, her lips swollen from my kiss and her eyes glazed with lust.

"Can you walk?" I asked after we were dried off.

"I think so," she said.

I smirked at her. "Then I still have work to do."

CHAPTER 11

Luna

"You finished it?" Zoe asked, her tone pitching with excitement as I held my phone to my ear.

I looked over the array of sketches I had strewn about all over our room, then at my opened laptop on the table across it. My website was fully designed, right down to an itemized shop for the pieces I already had in stock at my shop, and a whole section of my designs for pre-order. I was ready to hit publish, but I hadn't yet.

"I did," I finally answered her.

"Oh my gosh, I'm so pumped for you! I can't wait until you're home so we can celebrate."

I smiled, taking a seat at the table. Brad was at another function with Ezra, Ava, and their employees, continuing to get to know them while I'd utilized the time to put the finishing details on everything for my line.

"I haven't hit publish yet," I said.

"When are you going to?"

"I'm not sure," I admitted. "We still have eight days left at the retreat, so it's not like I could fulfil any of the preorders until then. If I get any."

"You'll get orders," she said confidently. God, I loved my friends. "Speaking of the retreat," she said, her voice going into full-gossip mode. "How *are* things going? You've been awfully quiet on the group text, no matter how many of us keep pestering you for details."

A flush raked my body, sending a warm tingle all the way down to my toes. If I was being honest, the last few days had been some of the best in my life, and not just because Brad was handing out orgasms like they were M&Ms. It was the role we were playing—a happy, healthy couple who went to fun functions and parties together, who relaxed and reminisced in bed together, who laughed together so much it made our sides hurt. A couple who couldn't keep their hands off each other.

It was everything I'd ever hoped for in a relationship...

But it wasn't real.

Brad was playing his role to perfection, just like he always had whenever he came up with these schemes. Hell, even in high school he'd had me pose as his girlfriend one time at a family political function so he could get out of yet another lecture from one of his parents' friends. He'd told them he had to take care of me because I had a cold, even though I'd been at my place, vegged out in front of the TV. He'd taken a picture to prove where he was at when his father questioned his sudden disappearance, his parents' friend never knowing I was just a friend.

"Okay, you've been silent way too long," Zoe said. "Now you *have* to tell me what's going on."

"Zoe," I groaned. It's not that I didn't want to share the last few days with her, I did. I trusted her as much as I trusted Brad, but it was the fact that I wasn't even clear myself on what was happening between me and my longtime best friend. Because while I could tell myself we were just playing a role all I wanted, I could feel it in my bones.

This wasn't a game to me.

It may have started that way, but the more time we spent together like we were—as a couple—I couldn't stop myself from wondering why we'd never tried it before.

"Come on," Zoe said. "Not only am I a badass psychologist, I can tell when you need to talk. Spill it."

I bit my bottom lip, wondering where to start.

"How about this," she said before I could respond. "If I tell you a mortifying secret you can never *ever* repeat, will you tell me what's going on between you and Brad?"

I sat up a little straighter in my chair. "You're Dr. Zoe Casson," I said. "Rule-follower and open-book extraordinaire. You don't have mortifying secrets." Seriously, the woman never made mistakes, it was uncanny.

"Oh stop it," she said. "I do too. And this one is *more than* worth whatever is happening at that resort."

"Okay," I said. "I'm more than intrigued. You tell me and I'll tell you." I didn't feel a hint of guilt about the quid-pro-quo because I knew Zoe would've never offered the tidbit if she didn't actually need to get it off her chest.

"You know the night of the masquerade party?"

"Yes," I said, remembering it vividly. It was only a week ago, and it happened to be the first time I kissed Brad.

"I may have...sort of...*possibly* slept with a stranger on the roof."

"You did what?" I blurted out the question, leaping out of my chair because the shock was way too much to take sitting down.

"I know," she groaned, and I could just picture her flailing her head back and covering her face with her hand. "I'm terrible. It was a mistake—"

"I think it's awesome!" I cut her off.

"What?"

"I mean, wait, was it good?"

She sighed, the sound almost nostalgic like she was

picturing some favorite memory of a blissful tropical vacation. "It was the best sex of my life."

"Omigod!" I squealed, practically doing a happy dance in the room. "How did it happen?"

"I don't know," she said. "We bumped into each other, one thing led to another, and before I knew it I was on the roof and he was..."

"On you!"

We both laughed before reeling it in.

"I saw you go up to the roof with a masked stranger! How the hell did you wait so long to tell me?"

"I don't know. It was so surreal and not like me at all. I blame the mask. It made me feel..."

"Like a different person?" I asked, totally understanding. That night had been all about shedding our inhibitions and taking a break from the stress of our daily lives.

"Exactly. And I haven't even told you the embarrassing part yet."

"What?"

"He was wearing a full-face mask," she explained, and I vaguely remembered it from the quick glimpse I got from the guy. "Like a super-hot one. It was silver and had all these cool markings on it, and he was wearing all black and his voice was super deep and I don't know what the hell came over me."

"Did you use protection?"

"Of course," she said.

"Then who cares? This is awesome!"

"It's mortifying. I don't do that. I don't even date, let alone have one-night stands. I don't even know his name. He put his number in my phone as Silver because that's what I kept calling him."

"You got his number—"

"He put his number in my phone," she cut over me.

"Has he texted?"

"Yep."

"Have you responded?"

"Nope."

"Why not?"

"Because, I slept with him on the roof of that club without even knowing his name! God, he could be literally anybody!"

"At least you know he wasn't anyone who met us there," I said. "You saw all their masks, and none were full-face-covering."

"I guess that's some relief, but there were a zillion people there. Jesus, I've never made a mistake that big."

"I didn't realize it was my turn to play therapist," I teased. "But why are you calling it a mistake? You used protection. You weren't drunk. You obviously had a good time. What's the bad?"

She huffed. "When you strip it down to just those details, nothing."

"Are you going to respond to his texts?"

"I don't know," she said. "I'm still trying to get over the mortification of my rash decisions. You know me, I don't break my own rules. And one I've always had is zero one-night-stands. Of course, I thought that was because I needed an emotional connection to have an orgasm, but that's obviously not true. The damn mask and not having sex in over a year made my instincts take over and tossed all my rules out the window."

"Well, I think it's a win. And good for you."

"Enough about me," she said, not at all casually putting the attention on me. "Your turn."

"I slept with Brad," I blurted out the words, somehow finding it much easier to say after she'd shared something so intimate with me.

"Yay!" she cheered.

"Seriously?"

"What? I love you both. I've seen it for years but neither of you ever acted on it."

"You never said anything!"

"I couldn't," she said. "You were with Dennis. Why would I put that in your head when I thought you were marginally happy with that dickwad?"

"Dickwad," I said, chuckling. "Is that a technical psychological term?"

"It is in my world," she said. "Now, how did it happen?"

I blew out a breath. "We're just playing our roles," I explained. "I'm his fiancé. And so we kissed a few times. Then Dennis texted something awful and Brad read it and he got up and sang my favorite song to make me smile while we were at a karaoke party and then..."

"And then?" she asked when I got lost in the memory.

"Then he took me back to our room and said he'd show me just how wrong Dennis was about everything. If I'd let him."

"And you let him!"

"And I let him."

"Holy shit this is the best day ever. How was it?"

"Best sex of my life," I echoed her earlier sentiment.

"I knew it!" she squealed. "You two have always had this fire between you."

I shook my head even though she couldn't see the denial. "We're friends," I said. "And again, these roles are temporary. That's all."

"Have you done it more than once?" she asked.

"Yes."

"That sounds like more than a role-playing thing to me."

"Does it?" I asked, honestly wondering. "Because we're here for eight more days. What happens when we get home? We'll go back to normal, right? Because it's not like we've talked about it. We've just been acting like we're engaged the whole time." I glanced down at the ring on my left hand, unable to stop the spread of warmth that radiated in my chest.

"How do you want it to be when you get home?" Zoe asked, going full psychologist mode.

"I don't know," I admitted. "It's hard to think about it."

"Fair," she said. "If you want things to change between you when you're home, you need to talk to him about it. If you're fine enjoying what's happening between you in this little pocket of safe adventure, then stick to it."

"You make it sound so easy," I said.

"It is."

"Okay, then text your mystery man."

"That's not the same thing."

"Isn't it? You're telling me to enjoy myself. Shouldn't you?"

She fell silent for a few seconds. "I'll think about it."

I smiled. "Then so will I."

"Look at us," she said. "Taking risks. I kind of like us in this mode."

"Me too," I said, laughing. "Miss you."

"Miss you too. Text me if you publish the site, okay? And text me if something more develops. And text me—"

"I'll text you," I said, stopping her ramble.

"Good. Love you."

"Love you too," I said before ending the call.

I glanced over my sketches that were all over the place and then my laptop that had fallen asleep while I was on the phone. I thought about what Zoe said, and tried to picture my life when we returned to Sweet Water. I closed my eyes and breathed deeply, letting whatever thoughts come to my mind without fighting them—Brad had told me to visualize the best, after all.

I saw my boutique. I saw orders piling in from my website. I saw myself going home after a long, successful day—

And Brad was there waiting for me. Smiling and wrapping his arms around me, greeting me with that kiss that sent me into orbit every single time. I saw us going to bed together and waking up together. I saw us taking trips together and grabbing dinner at *Lyla's Place* on Fridays. I saw us going on adventures together and binging Netflix together. I saw us laughing. I saw us—

Oh fuck me.

I was in love with him.

I snapped my eyes open, the revelation hitting me with the force of a truck.

I'd always loved Brad, that was easy to tell, but it felt like a part of me had always been *in* love with him but I'd never acknowledged it, and now that I did?

Shit, shit, shit.

I'd just gotten out of a relationship that was way worse than I'd even realized. And I was already in love? What if he didn't feel the same? What if we got home and he went back to being him—the smooth-talking, charming, playboy he'd always been?

How could I survive that?

How could I already be so entangled in him that my heart ached at the thought?

I set my phone on the table next to my laptop and shook my head at myself. I took a few deep breaths, and settled myself on focusing solely on the present. I could crumble and worry about everything in eight days. For now, I just wanted to revel in the bliss I'd been in seconds before I'd taken that visualization trip.

Because these last few days *had* been the best of my life, and I wasn't about to stop because I was worried about the future. Future me could deal with that. Present me just wanted to keep having fun, keep experiencing what it was like to be in a healthy relationship, real or not.

The front door opened, and Brad strolled in, his lips turning up in a smile when he spotted me. He scanned the array of sketches, some on the bed, some on the floor, a half-dozen on the table, and arched a brow at me.

"You've been busy today," he said.

"I have," I said, my heart racing at just the sight of him.

He peeled off his suit jacket, somehow the move looking sexier than when he stepped under the shower water completely naked.

Okay, maybe not *more*, but certainly equal.

God, I loved looking at him without any restraints. Loved looking at him and feeling like he was mine. What would've happened if we'd tried this for real years ago? What would our lives look like? We may very well be engaged if we worked this well together.

But did he want it to be real?

No. Nope. Nu-uh.

Present Luna needed to focus.

"How did the event go with the owners?" I asked after he'd rid himself of his tie, and crossed the room to me.

He slid a hand around my waist, tugging me to him and wrapping his arms around me. He sighed contently, like he'd been waiting to get me in his arms the entire morning. It made me light up from the inside out.

"Really well," he answered, pulling back just enough to look down at me. "Craig was there, constantly butting in, but that's to be expected. He's a smart investor, but has barely any tact. Either way, I like Ezra. Even if he doesn't go with me I feel like I've made a great acquaintance."

"I love that," I said, smiling up at him. "I have news too."

"What's up?"

"I'm finished."

He glanced around the room, then the sleeping laptop. "You're done?"

I nodded.

A smile spread over his lips. "Did you publish the site?"

I shook my head. "Not yet."

"When are you planning to?"

"Soon. I was hoping...only if you want to, of course..."

"Anything," he said when I hesitated.

"Maybe you could help me hire a marketing team? To help push it once I hit publish? I'll pay you back, of course. And we can draw up a contract if you want a percentage in the line."

"Done and done," he said, scooping me off my feet and spinning me around. "No contract. No percentage. I want to invest in you, solely for you."

Happy tears lined my eyes. "Really?"

"Really." He brought his lips to mine, brushing the barest of kisses over them. "I'm so fucking proud of you."

Heat radiated the length of my body, and I shifted in his embrace, locking my ankles behind his back while crushing my mouth against his. He groaned against the kiss, his hands shifting to my ass as he walked us toward the bed.

"Missed you all morning," he said between kisses as he laid me on the bed and settled himself between my thighs.

"Same," I said, frantically searching for his mouth again. I couldn't get enough of this man, I was practically starved for him. I went for the buttons of his shirt, undoing them quickly before pushing it off of his chest.

He took it off the rest of the way, leaning up to take mine off for me. We were a frenzy of kisses and touching, clothes flying this way and that until we were completely bare and he was between my legs again.

"Fuck, baby," he said, gliding his cock through my wetness. "Were you thinking about me like this?"

"Yes," I admitted, arching into his touch.

"I fucking love how responsive you are," he said, dipping his hard cock into my wetness before rubbing it over my sensitive clit. "Look at how you light up for me."

I pushed against his chest, nudging him over until he was on his back and I was on top of him. "Me?" I teased. "Look at *you*."

I kissed my way down his muscled chest, over his carved abdomen, until I hovered just over his cock. Anticipation and anxiousness swept over me, my body thrilling at the prospect of doing something new but my mind screaming at me that I didn't have a clue.

I'd never given a blowjob before, thanks to Dennis constantly saying foreplay was weak. But it had to be pretty basic right? I'd read enough romance novels to get the gist, but it didn't help my nerves one bit as I gripped his thick length with one hand and brought my lips to the head.

"Fuck," he groaned as I timidly wrapped my lips around him, flicking my tongue over his head as I explored the way he felt in my mouth. "*Luna*," he groaned as I took him deeper.

It wasn't easy. He was thick and long and big, and my mouth wasn't super accommodating. I used my hand to stroke what I couldn't get in, and bobbed up and down slowly. My heart raced in my chest, adrenaline crashing through me right alongside desire. I let instinct take over, giving into the way it felt to have him beneath me like this.

I pulled him out of my mouth, continuing to pump him as I dragged my tongue up his shaft and swirled it around his head. Then I carefully grazed my teeth over his length. He jolted, thrusting his hips upward.

"Is that okay?" I asked, totally worried I hurt him.

"Fuck yes," he groaned. "Baby, everything you do is perfect."

Warmth spread across my skin. "What about this?" I asked, flattening my tongue and taking him deep into my mouth before pulling him out again, using the wetness to glide my fisted hand around him more.

"Yes," he said.

"And this?" I sucked him into my mouth again, only to graze my teeth over him on the way back out.

"Fuck, do that again."

"Say please," I teased him like he had me in the shower the other day.

"Please, baby."

Damn, those words made me liquid.

I did it again. And again. I sucked him into my mouth, pumped him with my fist, and licked him until I found a rhythm that turned us both into a panting mess.

"Luna," he groaned, his thighs clenching beneath me. "If you keep doing that I'm going to come."

I didn't dare budge, didn't dare stop. I sucked at him harder, my mind whirling with sensation, with lust, with love as I took care of him like he had me so much this week. This... this was a delight. This was mutual passion and I couldn't get enough of it.

"Fuck," he groaned, hardening inside my mouth another degree before he spilled into me. I swallowed him down on instinct, the jolt of surprise passing quickly as I slowly pulled away to look down at him.

He reached up, cupping my cheeks before drawing me down against him, our bodies aligned as he took my mouth. No hesitation. No pause. He slid his tongue into my mouth, claiming me in a way that made me so damn achy.

"You're fucking incredible," he said, lightly nipping at my bottom lip before his blue-gray eyes filled with mischief. "My turn."

He flipped me over so fast I barely registered the change in position. My spine kissed the mattress, and he wasted no time kissing his way over my breasts, sucking and biting my nipples until they were rosy and peaked for him.

I tangled my fingers in his hair as he kissed his way over my stomach, never once speeding over my curves, instead taking his time worshiping every inch of me until I was so needy I whimpered.

He moved lower, wrapping his strong arms around my thighs and spreading them, hovering his face right over where I needed him most. "There's that beautiful pussy," he said, his warmth breath coating my sensitive flesh. "I've been thinking about tasting you all damn day."

His words made me shiver, made hot tendrils of desire course through my veins.

And then he licked up the center of me, the action like a match to gasoline.

I arched into his mouth, gasping at the sensation. I didn't think I'd ever get used to it, the feel of his tongue inside me. It was so intimate, so intense.

He lapped at me, alternating between thrusts and licks until my thighs clenched around his face, me rocking into his every lap.

"Mmm," he moaned. "You want control, baby?" he asked, but didn't wait for me to answer before he pulled away, rolling us until I was straddling his face.

"Brad!" I gasped, holding myself up above him. "What are you doing?"

He smiled up at me from between my thighs. "Sit."

"What?"

"Sit down."

"No, I can't. I'll crush you."

He cocked a brow at me. "Hands on the headboard," he said in that demanding way that had all of my nerve-endings standing at attention. Hell, who was I kidding, they were *singing* for him.

128

I did as I was told, gripping the headboard for leverage, but I still didn't drop down an inch.

"Luna," he chided. "I want you to ride my face until you come."

"Jesus," I moaned, unable to resist his words.

He gripped my hips, tugging me down until I was against his mouth.

"Omigod," I said, sighing as his tongue thrust inside me. I lifted up, but he pulled me back down, the sensation spinning my head. He licked at me from beneath, and my body melted into a puddle of pure desire. Pleasure built in my veins, rising and rising until it stretched beneath my skin.

I rocked against him, timidly at first, and then lost all reason because it felt so damn good.

"That's it, baby," he said, gripping my hips with just enough bite to make me even more slick. "Ride my face."

My entire body trembled as I rocked against his mouth, his tongue gliding against me as he ate at me while I moved above him. I felt him everywhere, between my thighs, underneath my body, his hands that held my hips and roamed over my skin. God, I couldn't get enough, I couldn't catch my breath, I couldn't—

"Brad!" I moaned his name as my orgasm tore through me, little shivers of delight spearing over every inch of my body. I gripped the headboard as I rocked and trembled through the intensity of it, barely able to breathe steadily as waves of pleasure rolled through me.

I lifted up once I was able to make sense of the world again, and Brad helped me, working me down his body until I could collapse on his chest.

"That was fucking beautiful," he said, licking my flavor off his lips.

I breathed deeply, slowing my racing heart as he held me. After a few moments, he shifted until I was on my side and he was facing me on his. He smoothed my hair away from my face, scanning every inch before meeting my eyes.

"You should take a nap," he said, likely noting the pure relaxed bliss in my eyes.

"Why is that?" I asked.

He smirked. "Because you haven't come on my cock today, and that's a necessity."

My lips parted, a zing of electricity snapping down the center of me. "Is it?"

"Absolutely."

"And if I told you I didn't need a nap?"

"Then I'd probably do something like this," he said, rolling us until he was on top of me, his cock hard and ready for round two as it slid between what he'd just made wet and slick with his mouth.

I gasped, my entire body feeling the sensation. I was *that* sensitive.

"You want more?" he asked, holding himself still at my entrance.

I shifted beneath him, spreading myself wider, giving him all the answer he needed.

"I don't think I'll ever get enough," I allowed myself to admit, knowing it was a risk to be so truthful but not finding the energy to care.

Something shuddered in Brad's eyes, something I couldn't read, and his mouth slanted over mine before I could wonder on it too long. Then he slid inside me, filling me, stretching me, and whisking me into a world of bliss I never wanted to surface from.

CHAPTER 12

Brad

"Fancy finding you four at my table," Ezra said as he took one of the available seats at the round-top we currently occupied in a private space they'd rented out in a local restaurant for tonight's dinner. Ava took the other, and Craig and Marla rounded out the rest.

"We were here first," I joked, accounting for Luna and myself as I stood up to shake Ezra's hand, then Ava's. We'd grown professionally friendly over the past few days, but I had no idea where we stood when it came to the business side, and surprisingly, that was okay with me.

Sure, I wanted them to pick me over Craig, but it was hard to worry about it when so much had happened in my personal life.

Luna sat next to me, saying her hellos to the couple and looking radiant as ever in a red cocktail dress that made her eyes pop. Fuck, she was so damn beautiful it was hard to pay attention to anything else. I couldn't believe she was on my arm, and that my ring was on her finger.

It's not real.

Well, the ring was real, but the engagement wasn't. I kept

having to remind myself of that fact, but it was hard as hell when the last few days had been unbridled bliss. I'd always had love for Luna, but I never knew how much until recently. Now that we'd crossed all the boundaries our friendship had in place, I never wanted it to end.

"Brad mentioned you had your own boutique in Sweet Water," Ava said, my name calling me back to the present as she spoke to Luna.

"I do," she said, beaming with pride. "It's one of the loves of my life."

Ava smiled, her eyes flashing to me. "I can guess the other."

Luna's eyes flared wide for a second before she returned her grin. "You'd be right," she said, shocking the hell out of me.

Fuck, did she mean that? I mean, I knew she loved me as a friend, that had never been a question. But was she still playing the role or was she being genuine? I hated that I didn't know. I really needed to remember that I was a damn adult and just ask her, but it felt unfair to do that with all she'd been through in the last few weeks.

"And a clothing line too?" Ezra asked.

"Yes," she said, flashing me a bashful look. "I'm planning on launching it soon."

"That's wonderful," Ezra said. "Let me know if you want to partner with our app. Brad showed me some of your designs. They're magnificent."

Her lips parted in shock, but I just shrugged. I loved talking about her and her work.

"Yes," Ava said. "Let me know when you launch the site. I'm dying to snag the leather jacket Brad showed me."

A beautiful flush raked over Luna's skin, but she nodded, and slipped her hand on my thigh beneath the table, squeezing it in what I assumed was a silent thank you.

"She made this suit too," I said, leaning back in my chair to better show it off.

"Brad," she quietly chided me.

"I love it," Ava said. "The blues and grays go so well with his eyes."

"Marla crochets," Craig said from my left. "She makes balloon animals out of them."

"That's fun," I said. "I donate to a local children's hospital in Charleston regularly. You'll have to give me your info so I can order some."

"Definitely," Marla said, a genuine smile on her face. It wasn't often Craig brought her into the conversation, so it was nice to see him acknowledge her without somehow making it about the pitch.

"We're a family of entrepreneurs," Craig said, eyes on Ezra. "And I'm all about growth. I think we could put you on a global level."

And there it was. Poor guy. His pushiness was making him look as desperate as he sounded.

"As you said yesterday," Ezra said before turning and ordering from the waiter.

Luna and I placed our orders as well, sharing a private look that was a barely contained laugh at how intense Craig was being. Ezra had heard most of our goals by now, and was doing his own research on who we were as people. There wouldn't be much more business that would sway him, but Craig didn't seem to pick up on that.

I laid my hand over Luna's beneath the table, inter-locking our fingers just because I could. I drew her hand up to my mouth, kissing the back of it before settling it back in my lap.

She smiled, and her chest rose and fell just a little faster, her cleavage on display in the sleeveless dress. And just like that, I was ready for dinner to be over.

A little while later, the waiter brought our orders and we fell into small talk while eating.

"You should come see her boutique sometime," I said after we'd finished eating.

Luna had been pretty much the sole focus as far as my conversation additives went, and I wasn't sorry for it. I couldn't help it, I was beaming with pride over all the hard work she'd done, and honestly, I never missed a chance to humbly brag about how damn amazing she was. Hell, I did that even before we'd fallen into...whatever it is we were now.

"We'd love to," Ava said. "I've always wanted to visit the smaller local towns. Sweet Water sounds like a slice of heaven."

"It is," I said, looking at Luna when I answered.

She bit her lip, barely containing her grin. God, this was too easy with her. Effortless and wonderful and I didn't want it to end. I always wanted to be the man putting that glow on her skin, that smile on her plump lips, that hint of desire in her eyes.

I kissed her hand again before excusing myself from the table, heading to the bathroom. Once I was finished, I washed my hands at the sink, only to find Craig there looking like he was waiting for me. He had a shit-eating grin on his face too.

"What is it?" I finally asked as I dried my hands.

"You're making this way too easy on me," he said.

"Excuse me?"

He shrugged. "When I heard it was the great *Brad Washbrook* I was up against, I thought you'd at least be a challenge."

"I'm not following you, Craig."

"You're blowing this deal."

"Oh really?" I asked, folding my arms over my chest. "What makes you say that?"

"All you can talk about is your fiancé," he said, snorting. "I haven't heard you offer Ezra one ounce of real equity you'd bring to his company the entire time we've been here. It's

Luna this and *Luna that*." He shook his head. "You might as well bow out and just enjoy the rest of the retreat."

I stepped closer to him, looking down because he was a good foot shorter than me. "Glad you think so," I said, smirking. "You keep playing your game, and I'll keep playing mine." I winked and spun around, heading out the door.

I waited until it shut before I lost the masked, confident smile I'd put in place. I hated to admit it, but what he said rattled me on the inside.

I *had* been talking about Luna more than I had the deal, but then again, Ezra knew where I stood from the private lunch we had. Still, I wasn't sure if Ezra and Ava understood the full value I could bring to their company, and I sure as hell hadn't been making an effort to shove it down their throats like Craig had either. I needed to find a balance, but I wouldn't apologize for being wrapped up in Luna.

And it was then that I realized while I *wanted* this deal, I didn't care if I lost it. All I wanted to do was focus on what truly mattered, and that was Luna.

Fuck, I was falling for her in a big bad way.

The fact was only further driven home when I came to the table, Luna standing there alone waiting for me, looking gorgeous as ever.

"Ezra and Ava went to dance," she said, motioning out of the private space to where the restaurant had a live band playing.

"Where's Marla?" I asked.

"She took off after Craig left."

I nodded, almost feeling sorry for her. Maybe if he paid her more attention than he did the business deal then she'd be here waiting for him like Luna had me.

"Dance with me?" I asked, and she looped her arm through mine as I led us to the dance floor.

The band played a slow, sultry tune, and Luna immediately wrapped her arms around my neck, swaying to the music.

I held her against me, relishing the way she felt in my arms. Something about having her here made me feel whole in a way I never knew possible, and it was really fucking hard to contain. I knew it wasn't fair, to spring my feelings on her when she'd just gotten out of a terrible relationship, but each day was getting harder and harder to keep my mouth shut.

Luna looked up at me, her eyes open and vulnerable, her smile real and so brilliant I had to reach between and trace my fingertip along the line of her lips.

"What's that smile for?" I asked.

"You," she said. "It's all for you."

My heart expanded in my chest, and I moved us to the music, the other dancers melting into the background as if it was just me and Luna on the dance floor.

"Remind me why we didn't do this sooner?" I asked, the question tearing through me.

Her eyes widened, but she shrugged. "I've been attached for years," she said. "And you've played the field for twice as long."

The truth stung, but I pushed past it. "I'd trade all those years if it meant I got a few more weeks with you like this."

Luna visibly swallowed. "Like what?"

I drew her closer, my lips an inch from hers. "Where you're mine."

Something serious and questioning flickered over her features, and I pressed my lips over hers before she could respond.

Call me a coward, but I couldn't take the rejection if she told me we were simply living out a fairytale with a rapidly approaching expiration date. And I wasn't fucking ready to turn into a pumpkin just yet.

CHAPTER 13

Luna

Zoe: Your leather jacket pre-order just sold out!

Anne: So did your cargo pants! I got one in every color!

Lyla: I snagged the white sundress before it sold out!

Happy tears lined my eyes as I read my friends' texts. I'd launched my site two days ago after Brad had hooked me up with his top marketing coordinator. They set me up on all the social media sites and we'd hit the ground running. All from the resort room. I couldn't believe it. Pre-order sales were slow the first day, but today all the marketing had come into play, and my friends were giving me minute-by-minute updates.

Me: You're all the freaking best. I owe you dinner when we get back!

Lyla: I'll close the place for you so we can celebrate with just us.

Anne: That sounds like a plan.

Zoe: I'm in.

Me: Thank you! I'll text you when we're on the road in a couple days.

I set my phone down, raking my hands through my hair

and telling myself to breathe. It was surreal. For so long I'd put off launching my clothes and my designs because Dennis had always said it would hurt when I failed. He'd been so sure I would too.

Damn, I felt like an idiot every time I looked back on the relationship. I hung on to who he'd been when we first started dating—charming and attentive—and ignored every red flag that I could now clearly see. Every time he passive aggressively complimented me—*you're cute, Luna, you don't need to try and look sexy.* Every time he put his needs in front of my own —*come on, you have a mountain of cash in your trust fund, I only need eight grand to invest in my buddy's business.* Every time he'd make it seem like I was asking for something outlandish sexually—*are you joking? You want me to dominate you? What bullshit book did you read that in?*

I clenched my eyes shut, shaking my head at myself. How was it that I'd let him make me believe all those things about myself? How did he manage to get such a hold on me?

Because you were loyal and hoped one day he'd change, hoped he'd go back to being who he was in the beginning. I knew better now. Knew I deserved better. Knew there were men in the world who believed in me, who treated me like royalty and worshiped me like a goddess...

Well, not men, but one man.

Brad.

He'd always believed in me, always made me smile, always put me first, and I knew nothing would ever compare to that kind of love.

Because it had to be love, right? There is no way he'd act like this, treat me like this for just the role. I couldn't believe that. I wouldn't.

My phone dinged again, and I scooped it up, fully prepared for it to be another update from my friends.

I was wrong.

Dennis: Saw your site. Don't let that shit go to your head. It's just a flash in the pan. What we had was real. I'll be right here when you figure that out.

Ugh. I rolled my eyes, pain streaking through me despite me telling myself he was full of shit. His texts were getting more frequent and bordering on cruel. I was over it. I hadn't been texting him back because I didn't want to give him the satisfaction, but I was so done.

Me: Stop texting me. We're done. Leave me alone.

Dennis: We'll never be done.

A cold shudder rolled through me reading those words, and I slammed my phone face down, not wanting to read another thing he might send.

I shook out my body like it would rid me of the creeps he'd given me, then assured myself he was just being his usual, arrogant, narcissistic self. All talk with no follow-through.

After a few deep breaths, I noted the time, and sprinted into action. Brad had been at events all day with the owners while I handled things on my website, and he was due back to our room in an hour. It gave me just enough time to order in dinner, change into a floral print skirt and blouse outfit I'd made a year ago, and set everything up on our balcony over-looking the ocean. I'd just finished bringing out our drinks when he walked into the door.

"You're home," I said, unable to contain the excitement rolling through me. I'd kept from texting him all day just so I could tell him everything in person.

"And you're stunning," he said, eying my outfit. "What's the occasion? Do I need to leave this on?" he asked, pointing to his suit jacket.

I shook my head, walking up to him and sliding the jacket off his shoulders before tossing it over the chair near us. "I have dinner," I said, motioning to the balcony before I loosened his tie and slipped it over his head. I took his hand and tugged him through the patio doors.

He surveyed the scene, noting the little table covered in takeout and drinks, the sun setting over the ocean beyond us.

"I don't deserve you," he said, dipping down to kiss me.

I melted into his embrace, opening for him as he slipped his tongue into my mouth, curling it against mine in a way that had tingles shooting down my spine. He broke away, grinning down at me before he took his seat and I took mine.

"Tell me," he said, no further explanation needed as he scooped up one of the tacos on his plate.

"I sold out."

"All of it?" he asked, a brilliant, prideful grin on his lips. "Not just one piece."

"All of it," I said, practically bouncing in my chair.

"I knew you would," he said. "I'm so proud of you."

"You didn't hire a bunch of people to buy my clothes, did you?" I asked before taking a bite of my taco.

He rolled his eyes. "You're joking, right?"

"I'm serious."

"Of course not," he said. "I wouldn't do that to you. Besides, you don't need me to. There was a market for your designs and you hit it."

I beamed, relief coiling through me. "I couldn't have done any of this without you," I said. "The tacos are a poor thank you, but it's a start."

"Don't do that," he said, finishing off a taco and diving in for the next. "This is all you. I may have hooked you up with a marketer, but it was your designs that sold out. Your clothes. Your line. Nothing else."

Happiness fluttered through me so much I swore I could fly right off this balcony and into the sky if he asked me to.

We ate and chatted about his day in something that felt

utterly domestic but totally natural and fun at the same time. I could probably do this forever and never get tired of it.

After we finished eating, I cleaned up our plates while Brad grabbed a bottle of champagne and popped the cork, pouring us two glasses to celebrate. We took them back out to the balcony, settling into our chairs with the bottle between us on the table. The sun had fully set, leaving the sky an inky midnight with sparkling stars scattered across it. The ocean waves crashed below us, the sound the perfect backdrop to one hell of a perfect day.

"To your success," Brad said, clinking his glass against mine.

"To ours," I said before we both took a sip. The liquid was crisp and fresh on my tongue, the bubbles going straight to my head.

"I hope they choose me," he said, referring to his portion of the success I mentioned. "But as much as I hate to admit it, Craig has some viable assets to offer them. I feel like it's a coin toss."

I furrowed my brow. "I don't see it. He's so...pushy."

Brad shrugged. "Not up to me," he said. "I've done pretty much all I can."

"Then that's all that matters," I said, setting down my glass. "I would definitely choose you."

"I don't believe you," he said, his tone playful.

I gaped at him. "Why not?"

He shrugged, putting on a faux pout. "Because you're all the way over there and I'm all the way over here."

A laugh tore from my lips and I shook my head as I pointed to the table between us. "This is like two feet wide."

"Facts are facts."

I rolled my eyes. "You're a big baby," I said, getting up and crossing the very small distance between us. "This better?"

"Nope," he said, his hands trailing up my thighs beneath my skirt as I stood before him.

"What would be better?" I asked, my pulse thrumming in my veins.

"This," he said, and tugged me forward until I straddled his lap, bringing us chest to chest and face to face.

I wrapped my arms around his neck. "This close enough?"

He slid his hands beneath my skirt, massaging my thighs in a savoring way that sent warm chills across my skin. "No," he said, brushing his lips over mine.

I laughed again, kissing him back. "I don't think we could be any closer."

"Oh, we could."

"How so?"

"You could let me fuck you right here on this balcony, where anyone might see."

A thrill of heat shot right through me, an ache pulsing between my thighs.

"That would be close enough?" I asked, my voice a little breathless.

"Only one way to find out," he said, his eyes full of heat and challenge and *damn* did it do things to my body.

"I guess it would be easy," I said, heat flushing my cheeks. He tilted his head, and I reached for his hand, guiding it higher beneath my skirt.

"Fucking hell, baby," he said, his fingers meeting my bare heat. "You're a little vixen, aren't you? Having dinner with me this whole time and never telling me you had nothing beneath this skirt."

I grinned. "I figured you'd find out sooner or later."

"It's later," he said, shifting beneath me to unzip his pants.

In a few moves, he was free of the restraints, his hard cock teasing me beneath my skirt, which still covered everything. It was exhilarating, feeling so intimate while also being completely exposed. I very quickly realized I loved it, craved it, and couldn't be happier that Brad was so into it too. It was like we were matched on every single level.

He slid an arm around my lower back, urging me forward. "Fuck," he groaned. "You're so slick."

I shivered as I slid over his hard length, the heat and pressure making me come alive with need.

"I missed you all day," I said, capturing his lips with mine. I kissed him hard, rocking against him without taking him fully inside me. I was having too much fun with the tease. "It was so hard not to text you with the news."

He groaned as I rolled my hips over him, his hand flexing on my hip as he slid his tongue against mine. "Tell me," he said. "Always tell me. Never wait, baby."

I gasped when his other hand moved beneath my shirt, cupping my breast over the lace. "I didn't want to bother you," I admitted, having a really hard time keeping up with the conversation while he was touching me.

He pinched my nipple enough for it to sting, making me whimper before he leaned down, lifting my shirt enough that he could soothe the hurt with his tongue. "You'd never bother me," he said, pulling the lace down to glide his tongue over the peaked bud. He urged me forward again with that hand on my back, pressing me against him harder, faster. "I could be in the most important meeting of my life, and you could call to tell me what you ate for lunch, and I wouldn't be bothered."

I trembled, his words going straight to my head right along with his touch. My body was a live wire he was playing like a mastered instrument.

"Brad," I sighed his name, tangling my fingers in his hair so I could draw his mouth back up to mine.

He released my shirt, letting it fall back in place as he gently gripped my chin, taking hold of the kiss. He swept into my mouth with his tongue, keeping that firm grip, directing my mouth in whatever way he wanted to kiss me deeper. It was purely animalistic, and it made me liquid as I rocked against him.

Brad tipped my head back, his lips meeting my neck before he lightly bit me. I gripped his hair in response, and he growled from the sting. The stars stretched wide above us, the cool night air kissing my flushed skin as he bit me again, harder this time.

"God, yes," I moaned, rocking harder against him.

"Enough teasing me," he groaned, kissing the small hurts on my neck. "Put my cock inside you, my hands are occupied."

The demand rippled through me, just as the light smack on my ass did with one hand in question.

I reached between us, beneath my skirt, and gripped his length, guiding him to my entrance. I played with him for a few more seconds, teasing my throbbing clit with his head before he growled again.

"Do that again," I begged, and his eyes locked with mine.

A smirk shaped his perfect lips before he growled again, the sound reverberating right down to my bones it was so fucking sexy.

I sank atop him with one fast, smooth motion, and relished the flare in his eyes as I took him all the way to the hilt.

For a few seconds, we remained still, holding each other's gazes. He filled me so much I could hardly breathe around the sensation, and I pulsed around him, my body begging me to *move*.

Brad trailed his hand over the line of my jaw, the look in his eyes just this side of adoring and absolutely starved. It was enough to make me breathless, make me wants things I had no business wanting—like making this my forever.

Then he leaned in and kissed me so softly and with such intention, I almost cried. I clung to him, bringing our bodies flush as I wrapped my arms around his neck. Without breaking the kiss, I rolled my hips, slowly, deliberately.

Brad groaned into my mouth, his hands flying to my hips as I rocked against him. "Fuck, baby," he said against my lips. "You feel so damn amazing riding my cock."

"You like that?" I asked, rolling my hips for emphasis.

"Love it," he said, sucking my bottom lip into his mouth.

I shivered with delight, all my senses firing. His touch was searing, and the sound of the ocean crashing behind us only reminded me of how very out in the open we were. There were other villas with balconies that could easily see ours, but somehow, that made this all the more exciting. And who fucking cared if someone saw us? Everything was covered, no one would be able to tell what was going on beneath my skirt—which was *a lot*.

I upped my pace, my nails digging into his shoulders as I rode him harder, faster, giving in to my body's demands as my pleasure swirled and shivered in my veins.

"God, you're beautiful," he said, eyes scanning the length of my body as I rode him. "Look at you. All breathless and needy. Chasing your release. Fucking love it. Love..." He groaned, his words cutting off as he thrust into me from below, adding to the chase.

"Brad," I moaned his name, and his hand flew up to cover my mouth. The sensation sent me spiraling, the dominance in it a sharp, blissful thing.

"See if you can come without screaming my name, baby," he said, nothing but pure pleasure in his eyes.

I rocked into him harder, relishing the look on his face as he tried to hold in his noises too.

"Fuck," he hissed, dropping his hand from my mouth only to replace it with his lips. He kissed me hard and fast and hungry, both our bodies tensing as we crashed together, racing toward that sharp edge. "Luna," he moaned into my mouth.

I kissed him right back, whimpering into the kiss as my release shot down my spine, my muscles trembling with the intensity of it as a million little tingles erupted beneath my skin. Brad kissed me harder, his release following mine as he hardened inside me another degree before he spilled into me.

We caught our breath between kisses, slowing as our bodies trembled from the pleasure as we came down. I leaned my forehead against his, relief and appreciation flooding my entire being until I laughed softly.

"What is it?" he asked, his voice laced with pleasure.

"You never make me feel bad about this kind of thing."

"What kind of thing?"

I rocked against him for emphasis. "For wanting you like this. For needing you on this level."

He drew back, cupping my face again. "The only thing I ever want to do is make you happy, make you feel good."

"You do," I said. "You have no idea how much you do."

Our gazes locked, and the words were beating out a rhythm in my heart.

I love you, I love you, I love you.

But I couldn't say them, couldn't bring them to the tip of my tongue. I was terrified he wouldn't feel the same. Terrified this was all just a game, a role, a fun experiment. So, coward that I was, I kept my mouth shut, and wished on every star above us that I'd find the courage to tell him before our time was up.

We only had two more days, but I knew that even a lifetime with him wouldn't be enough.

CHAPTER 14

Brad

"And the stand-out employee award goes to Sara Stone," Ezra announced from his position on the stage, Ava standing next to him holding a stack of envelopes in her hands.

The employee in question smiled and headed up to the stage, gratefully taking the envelope Ava offered her before hugging them both and heading back to her table to the sound of applause.

Ezra continued with the awards, handing a unique and tailored award to half his employees. This entire retreat had been a company award in its own right, and the last party of the event was nothing short of epic. The ballroom had been transformed into an eighty's throwback extravaganza, complete with bursts of neon colors over every available surface, disposable cameras at every table, and more than a few retro-style glasses and accessories to pick from to wear.

Everyone was dressed accordingly, myself and Luna included. I wore a button-down shirt that was speckled with flecks of white and gray with bright teal, pink, and yellow shapes over it. Luna looked downright ravishing in a wide-leg jumpsuit that was constructed of a million little sequins all sectioned off in bright colors of blue, yellow, green, and pink. Her shoulders were bare, the neckline plunging just shy of her cleavage, and her long red hair was in this irresistible messy tease that rose off her head before cascading down one shoulder.

She took my breath away no matter what she was wearing, and I knew I needed to tell her. I needed to tell her that I'd fallen for her, that I loved her, that I didn't want *us* to end just because tonight was the last night of the retreat.

"I've spoken to each of you individually," Ezra continued after all the awards had been handed out, drawing my thoughts to the present. "So I know you all understand the level of admiration, pride, and appreciation I have for each and every one of you. Close-to-Custom wouldn't be the company it is without your hard work and dedication, and I hope that this little vacation from the regular nine-to-five has shown you that. Our little company started with a dream of bringing better fits to the masses, and it's grown exponentially in the past year. Even with that being said, Ava and I both know there is more ground to cover." Ezra glanced at me, flashing me a knowing look that made hope course through my veins. "We believe expansion is on the rise with the prospects of new investors," he continued, winking at me before returning his gaze to the audience as a whole. "And that means we'll have more growth opportunities for you, for the brands we work with, and more." He turned to Ava, interlocking their hands before facing the audience once more. "Thank you all for a fantastic year. Let's enjoy the hell out of our last night of vacation!"

The crowd erupted with applause, almost everyone standing to clap as Ezra and Ava descended from the stage and *Take On Me* by a-ha took over the sound system.

"Cheers," Luna said, tapping her glass against mine.

I echoed the move before sipping the icy red cocktail in my glass. "What's this called again?" I asked, glancing around our table for the card that explained all the themed cocktails.

"Woo woo," Luna said. "It's yummy. Perfect for celebrating your success."

I laughed, watching as she took another sip. She licked a few stray drops off her lips, and I swallowed hard. Fuck, she was sexy. And funny and smart and talented. The complete package.

"Nothing is solid yet," I finally managed to say.

"Please," she said, waving me off and setting down her drink. "Did you see the wink? Ezra is very Team Brad."

I grinned at her. "What about you?"

"What about me?" she asked.

"What team are you on?"

She bit back her smile. "That depends."

"On?"

She nodded toward the dance floor where throngs of people were dancing. "On if you'll dance with me or not."

"Always." I pushed away from the table, offering her my hand.

She took it, sliding hers into mine and allowing me to lead her through the crowd until we found a spot. I wrapped my arms around her, bringing her body flush against mine as we moved to the music.

Luna grinned up at me, laughing with each song change as we adjusted to the melody. It was effortless and fun as hell. And her smile, the sound of her laugh, was *everything*. My heart couldn't get any fuller. I had the girl of my dreams in my arms, the smell of her skin still lingering on mine from the way I'd claimed her body earlier, and she'd let me help her launch her clothing line, a dream she'd had for years. Not to mention I was pretty sure Ezra would be signing with me before the night was over.

Everything was perfect.

But I needed to know Luna was really *with* me. Needed to know she wasn't simply playing her part for my benefit. And as much as I knew I needed to give her time because of her recent breakup, I also knew there was no way I could go home and just pretend to be her friend again. If she told me that was what she needed while she healed, then fuck yes, I'd do it. I'd wait for her forever, but I needed to know where her mind was at, even if it wasn't fully Team Brad like she'd mentioned earlier.

I parted my lips, ready to lay all my cards out in front of her—

"I need a break!" she said over the music, waving behind her. "Bathroom. Meet you back at the table?"

A rush of breath flew past my lips, all the buildup of my confession delayed with her words. I nodded, grinning at her before she turned around and weaved through the crowd and out of the ballroom, headed for the bathrooms just outside of it.

I watched her the entire time, moving through the dancers until I stood by our table and she was out of sight.

"You're a real piece of work, Washbrook," Craig's voice sounded from behind me, so I shifted to face him. From the glare shaping his face, he was a little more than pissed. "I don't know what you offered him that I didn't, but it seems beyond business. I think they like you more for your fiancé than your investment interest."

His words were slightly slurred, and I did my best to take that into account as I cooled the instant anger that boiled in my gut. I took a deep breath and shook my head.

"Nothing is official yet," I said. "But you're not giving them any credit if you think they're basing it off my relationship status."

"Bullshit," he fired back. "You and Luna have been all over

them. Attending all the events, the couply shit, getting more time—"

"And you and Marla haven't?"

Craig shrugged. "I didn't force Marla to attend everything."

"I didn't force Luna either," I said, then felt a flare of guilt shoot through me. In a way, I had forced her into this entire situation, concocting a fake relationship so I could get more time, but that had been mainly in the beginning. Everything since day two had felt more real than any relationship I'd ever had.

But I didn't know if it felt real for her.

Fuck, I really needed to find out.

"Whatever," Craig grumbled. "Something feels off about you."

I rolled my eyes. "That's understandable when you come in last place."

"Fuck you, Washbrook," he said, draining the contents of his drink.

I shook my head, holding my drink up to him as he stumbled away, flipping me off in the process. I took a sip of my drink, forcing his words away. He could be pissed all he wanted. It couldn't touch me.

Not tonight.

Not after I'd spent two perfect weeks with Luna on my arm and in my bed, filling my head with nothing but blissful hope for a future that looked brighter than any before.

All I had to do was talk to her, and hope to hell she felt the same way.

CHAPTER 15

Luna

I washed my hands before surveying myself in the mirror. Two months ago, I would've never been wearing something like this—a themed outfit for a party that was beyond fun. Because all my attempts to have little adventures like this were always shut down.

But not anymore.

Not with Brad.

He hadn't even hesitated when I showed him the totally cheesy and one-hundred-percent eighties shirt I'd gotten for him to wear tonight. He'd smiled at me, said *hell yes*, and thrown it on. And he looked damn good wearing it too, adding a pair of almost too tight black pants with it and some neon sneakers. He was so relaxed about everything, so eager to have fun. I never had to worry that he'd say my idea was stupid or that I was reaching when asking for the most basic of things.

And I hadn't realized how much I'd craved that in my life until we came on this trip. Until Brad showed me that there were people in the world who didn't overreact to every little inconvenience or even the smallest of requests on my end—

like a fun dinner or movie night. Until he showed me that there were people in the world who actually took an interest in what excited me, what brought me joy.

I had no idea how I'd never seen it before, how I'd never allowed myself to feel the chemistry that radiated between me and my best friend, but I was more than determined to not waste another second denying it.

Tonight was our last night here, and I was terrified that everything would change between us on the plane ride home. But I wouldn't live in fear. I would tell him tonight. Tell him how much these past two weeks had meant to me, how much him allowing me to be *me* without judgment or reproach had helped me find myself again. Helped me realize that I'd been living in a dark cloud of doubt and pain for way too long. Helped me figure out where my heart had been all along —with him.

Was it fast? Yes. I knew that. And I knew there was a chance he didn't want a real relationship with me, but I wasn't going to let that stop me from telling him the truth. He deserved to know how crazy in love I was with him, and how amazing he was and had always been to me. He deserved so much more than I had to offer, but I hoped he'd give me a chance to earn his love in return.

Excitement and anticipation fluttered through me, making me feel tingly all over as I pushed through the bathroom doors, determined to find Brad and tell him right then and there. If anything, it would stop the *what-if* game I kept playing in my head and that would be a relief—

"You blocked my number."

My blood ran cold with the sound of Dennis's voice, and I stopped in my tracks as he rounded the corner just outside the lady's room.

"And my email," he said, his eyes narrowed as he looked down at me, blocking my way ahead.

"What the hell are you doing here?" I snapped, adrenaline coursing through my veins and making my fingers tremble. "How did you *know* I was here?" I amended when I realized the fucking odds of him being in Myrtle Beach, at this resort.

"You blocked me," he said, like that was more than enough of an answer. "How else was I going to get you to listen?"

"How did you *find* me?" I asked again, my breathing harsh.

"That's all you have to say to me?" he asked, stepping closer, reaching for me. I jerked away from his touch, and he put his hands up. "I came here for you. I came *all* this way for you, Luna. I've been a wreck without you. I've told you that, but you wouldn't respond, wouldn't listen. You're going to listen now."

"The hell I am," I snapped, then moved to step around him. He blocked my path, and all the hairs on the back of my neck stood on end. "Move."

"No," he said, planting his feet. "You need to listen to me."

"No, I really fucking don't," I said, meeting his eyes. "You cheated on me, not the other way around. And I'm honestly shocked you're acting like you ever cared about me," I continued, the floodgates opened. "You constantly put me down. Constantly manipulated me into thinking you were some goddamn hero and that I should be honored that you'd want to be with me." I rolled my eyes at myself. I'd been such an...

No. I would not degrade myself for this asshole. He's the one to blame, he's the one that gaslit my world until all I could see was him, and I was done. So very done.

"We're over. I will never listen to your excuses, your pleas, or whatever the hell you're trying to do. Leave me alone." I shoved past him faster than he could block me, air filling my lungs as I almost jogged toward the ballroom. I wanted to get back to the life I'd been living, get back to Brad and the safety and comfort of his presence.

I cleared the ballroom doors, my heart racing in my chest as I beelined it toward our table—

A hand grabbed my arm, jerking me around so quickly I nearly lost my balance. Pain radiated up my arm as I tried to tug it out from Dennis's grasp. "Let go!" I shouted, but the loud, thumping music swallowed my plea.

"No," he snapped, jerking me toward him. "Not until you listen to me!"

Ice shot through my veins, making my entire body shake. He'd never been violent with me before—though I couldn't say the same for the holes he'd sometimes punch in the walls. I took a deep breath, trying like hell to calm my nerves.

"Dennis," I said, using every ounce of power I had to fill my voice. "Let me go. You're hurting me."

He grip loosened, but he didn't let me go. "It's not the same without you," he said. "I need you back."

I tried to free my arm again, but he kept ahold of me. "You don't want me back," I said. "And I'm not coming back either way."

"I do want you back," he argued. "I didn't care about that other girl. I never did. It was just a release. And I'm behind on my rent, I need your help—"

"Money," I cut him off, laughing darkly. "Of course, it's about money." I'd helped him out more than I should've. Clearly. "Let go."

"No. I'm here for you to remember how much you love me. How great we were together—"

"Get your fucking hands off her," a loud, angry, primal voice sounded from right behind me.

One second, Dennis was holding my arm, not letting me go, and the next, Brad's fist was connecting with Dennis's jaw.

CHAPTER 16

Brad

White-hot pain zapped across my knuckles as my fist met Dennis's face, but I barely registered the pain as he whirled from the hit, releasing Luna's arm so quickly she stumbled back a few steps.

A blink and I was there, steadying her, running my hands over her face and body. "Did he hurt you?" I asked, relief on the edge of my soul noting she had no tears in her eyes and barely any fear.

"No," she said, swallowing hard. "Not really. Just my arm when he grabbed me."

I saw red, spinning around and stomping toward where he was getting back to his feet—

"Brad!" Luna's voice was a plea I would never be able to ignore, my entire body locking up on instinct as she sprinted ahead of me, hands splayed on my chest. "Please," she said. "He's not worth it." She reached down, skimming her fingers over my knuckles. "Are you okay?"

"I'm fine," I said, finally focusing on her. "I'm worried about you."

A crowd was gathering around us now as Dennis straightened his spine. "Asshole," he said, working out his jaw. He noted the way I tugged Luna behind me, then glared at me. "I knew you and her were always fucking behind my back. Typical," he fired, looking around me at Luna. "You're such a hypocrite."

"*Leave,*" Luna said from behind me.

I furrowed my brow, my hands fists at my sides. "How the fuck are you here, anyway?" I asked, knowing damn well the only people who knew about me and Luna attending this event were our closest friends, and they'd never tell him.

"She wants me here," Dennis said, jabbing a finger toward Luna. "That's how."

"That's not true!" Luna said, stepping to my side to look up at me. "I blocked his number—"

"And yet you're still allowing me to track your location," Dennis cut her off.

My lips parted in shock as I looked down at Luna.

"Omigod," she gasped, shaking her head. "I forgot," she said quickly. "I forgot to turn it off—"

"How could you forget something like that?" I asked, furious at Dennis and terrified for her. What if he'd found her and I hadn't been here? What if he'd tracked her down and the situation escalated to something worse. Fuck me, just the idea of her being hurt had my entire body shaking.

"I..." Luna stumbled over her words, shock and hurt coloring her features.

"It's because she wanted me here!" Dennis snapped, digging in his phone. He pulled up a picture, one of him and Luna kissing from just last month and shoved it in my face. "Because she missed me. That's why she left it on. She didn't want to be here with you—"

"Brad?" Ezra's voice sounded from behind me, and I

turned just in time to see him shoving through the crowd to survey the scene. His eyes widened at the photo. "What's going on?"

"I'm here to get my girlfriend back," Dennis said. "Who the hell are you?"

"This is my event," Ezra said coolly. "And I don't remember handing you an invitation."

Craig was the next person to shove through the crowd, nothing but malicious intrigue lighting up his eyes as he spotted the photo Dennis still held up. "That's from three weeks ago," he said, reading the timestamp above the damn photo and almost bouncing on his feet with delight. "Holy shit, this whole engagement stuff you've been spouting with her has been fake!"

"Engaged? Those two?" Dennis shook his head. "No way. We've been together for years."

"We're done!" Luna fired his direction, stepping toward him like she might strangle him. I held out an arm, gently holding her back.

"Wow," Craig said, nodding to Ezra. "Do you really want to get into business with a liar?"

Ezra pursed his lips, looking at me. "Are you with Luna or not?"

I swallowed the knot in my throat, my mind whirling. Instinct shouted at me to pummel Dennis for even trying to come near Luna again, but the uncertainty of where we stood haunted my every breath.

"I'm not," I finally breathed the answer, and hated the gasp that slipped past Luna's lips.

Shit. Had she wanted me to lay claim to her when we hadn't ever discussed the reality of our situation? I didn't want to speak for her without her telling me exactly what she wanted. Fuck me, I shouldn't have waited so long—

Luna shoved past me, through the crowd, hurrying out of the ballroom.

"Luna!" I called after her, moving to follow her.

"That's right," Dennis said, stepping in front of me. "She'd never pick you. Not when she could have me. Not when I've been inside her more times than you could ever imagine—"

I didn't think, didn't breathe, I reacted.

My fists stung, my knuckles singing as I hit and hit and *hit*.

"You never treated her right!" Punch, crack. We tumbled to the floor, and I hit him again, feeling him go limp beneath me. But I wasn't going to stop. I wasn't going to stop until I'd paid back every ounce of pain he'd ever caused her—

Arms encircled me from behind, dragging me off the floor, forcing me to stand before shoving me through the crowd that parted with nothing but fear in their eyes. I heard Ezra give a few demands to his security team before he shoved me into the hallway, down it a bit, and into a room before he slammed the door behind us.

"My team will get that asshole to the police," Ezra said, and my vision finally cleared of red.

We were in a small conference like room, Ezra leaning against the closed door as if he was afraid I'd bolt through it and attack Dennis again.

I breathed deeply, urging the adrenaline to slow it as I shook out my aching hands. Fuck, I had blood on my knuckles that wasn't mine.

"I'm sorry," I finally said to Ezra. "I wasn't trying to scam you," I explained. "I just wanted a fair shot at your time."

"Who is Luna to you?" he asked, calmer than me for sure.

"Everything," I said. "She's everything to me. And I respect you, Ezra. I really fucking do. You know that. You know how I feel about your company, but if it comes down to this business deal or chasing after the girl of my dreams, then you know what I'll choose."

"Her."

"It will always be her," I said, stepping up to him. "Please move."

Ezra nodded, grinning up at me as he stepped to the side. "Go get her."

CHAPTER 17

Luna

I didn't even bother getting my things from our room—I just headed right out of the hotel lobby and hailed a cab with nothing but my small clutch in my hands and tears streaming down my cheeks.

Lucky for me, I had my wallet and phone in my clutch, and it was all too easy to make it to the airport and buy a ticket home. I'd have to wait an hour, but who cared? I'd absolutely ruined *everything* in the span of ten minutes.

I sat heavily in the waiting area for my flight, hurrying through my phone to turn off the tracking app. I hadn't even thought about it after I'd blocked him, certain that it would take care of the sharing information portion of my phone too. Apparently not.

Not only did it lead him right to me, but it'd exposed what Brad and I had done, the relationship we'd concocted.

Dennis may have showed up and wrecked everything, but *I'd* lost the deal for Brad. Lost it by ever being connected to a person like Dennis. Lost it because Dennis wouldn't have even been there if I hadn't blocked his number, hadn't stopped responding to his antics.

Tears flowed freely now, the loss hitting me dead center in the chest. Not only had I ruined things for Brad's potential business deal—which would've been in the millions for him— I lost *him*. He'd been more than clear when he stated we weren't really together, and as much as that broke my heart, the idea that I'd pushed away my best friend hurt just as much. Because I'd known the stakes when we playfully crossed that line and I'd ignored them. There was no way I'd ever be able to look at Brad with anything but the intense love I had for him, no way I'd be able to go back to being just friends.

And hell, after everything I'd cost him, he probably wouldn't want to anyway.

I ignored the looks from other passengers waiting on the flight, both surveying my eighties outfit and my tears, and focused on my phone, pulling up my group text.

Me: Who wants to pick me up from the airport at three a.m.?

It was mainly a joke, but the need to talk to my girls was overwhelming as my heart crumbled.

Zoe: What happened to Brad's plane?

Me: He's still at the retreat. I needed to get away.

Anne: What happened?

I gave them the quickest version of Dennis showing up to ruin my life once again, but really, I was the one to blame.

Lyla: Asshole.

Anne: Need me to get my father's plane? We can be on it with shovels in two seconds.

Zoe: I'll bring the tarp.

Lyla: I'll work on the alibi.

A watery laugh slipped by my lips as the support from my friends filled the painful cracks in my soul.

Me: I'm okay, but thank you. And I was kidding about the ride. I'll grab a Lyft. I just wanted to talk.

Zoe: We'll be here when you get home.

Lyla: Want to meet at my place?

Anne: I'll bring wine.

Me: You all are the best. But I just want to crawl into my bed and hide for a few days.

Zoe: Fair.

Anne: Fine, but after.

Lyla: Definitely.

Me: Love you guys.

They all echoed their sentiments, and I stashed my phone, content to lean back and shut my eyes while I waited. But before I could even think about trying to simply breathe for a few moments, I spotted *Brad* racing through the airport, heading straight for my gate.

I leaped out of my seat, gaping at him.

"Where are you going, Luna?" he asked, totally out of breath as he skidded to a stop in front of me.

"*Me*? What are you doing here?" I fired back. "You should be trying to fix the deal I ruined—"

"Fuck the deal," he cut over me. "Where are you *going*?"

"Home," I said. "Where I can't cost you a fortune. Where I can't want things from you I shouldn't."

"I don't care about the deal," he said again. "I don't care about the money." He stepped toward me, reaching out to slide his hand around the back of my neck. "All I care about is you."

I trembled at his touch, leaning into it as tears rolled down my cheeks. "Brad," I said, trying like hell to breathe. "I can't keep up the act," I admitted. "I can't. It's killing me."

Brad arched a brow at me, cupping my cheeks and swiping away my tears with the pads of his thumbs.

"I can't keep pretending like everything that's happened between us isn't real," I said.

"And I can't keep pretending like we're going to go home and go back to normal," Brad said.

"Isn't that what you want?" I asked.

"Fuck no," he grumbled, shaking his head. "I want you, Luna. I want adventures and trips and boring nights at home. I want to argue over where we should order dinner from or what show we want to binge. I want you in every aspect of my life—my days and my nights and everything in-between. You're my best friend, Luna. My love, my inspiration, my fucking everything."

My heart thumped wildly at his words, at the way he leaned down, his lips hovering an inch above mine.

"I want all of you," he whispered, holding me there in the sweetest anticipation.

"You do?" I asked, totally shocked and baffled that this amazing, intelligent, funny, passionate man wanted me in all those ways.

"I do," he said. "Then. Now. Always."

"I love you." The words rushed from me on an exhaled breath and it felt like I'd been holding them in for years. "I love you so much," I continued. "I thought I was going to lose you, thought I'd ruined everything."

"You love me?" he asked, his blue-gray eyes guttering.

"So damn much," I answered.

"I love you too," he said, dipping down to capture my lips with his. "So, where are you going?" he asked, pulling back enough to catch my gaze.

"Wherever you want to take me," I answered.

* * *

"You know," Brad said after he'd cleaned up in the bathroom back at our resort room.

My lips were still swollen from the amount of kissing we'd done in the back of the Lyft, but bless that driver, he hadn't said a word. I'd texted the girls to say not to wait up or worry about me, and filled them in on what I'd learned about Dennis —that he'd scurried back home after Ezra threatened to have him arrested for trespassing. "I think it's a good thing."

"What?" I asked.

He turned to face me, pure mischief rippling over his features. "That we had our first fight."

I bit back a laugh. "That was more of a heartbreak moment than a fight," I said, my body and soul still reeling from the way the night had turned. I went from thinking I'd ruined and lost everything to being handed the greatest gift on the planet—*him*.

"Either way, we get to make up now."

Warmth shot down my spine at his words, at the look in his eyes as he reached for me. He slid his hands around my hips, gently turning me until my back was facing him. He kissed my neck, then over my bare shoulder as his fingers made their way up to the zipper of my jumpsuit.

"May I?" he asked, the formal, polite question making anticipation flare in my core.

I never knew if he was going to be dominant or submissive, gentle or rough, and I *loved* the thrill of finding out which version I'd get each time. It was easy when I loved them all.

"Yes," I said, chill bumps erupting over my skin as he dragged the zipper down the line of my spine.

The suit loosened around my body, and he gently slid the straps off my arms until all the fabric fell down my body and pooled at my feet. I wiggled out of my heels, then stepped out of the fabric, all while he trailed a line of kisses down my spine that had my blood thrumming in my veins.

"Luna," he said, spinning me to face him. "I'm sorry."

I furrowed my brow. "I'm the one who's sorry," I countered.

"No," he said, trailing his fingertips along every inch of my bare skin, teasing my breasts over the lace covering them. "I'm sorry I held it back so long."

I swallowed hard, my heart thumping against my chest.

"Sorry I didn't just tell you how I felt," he said. "It would've prevented all of this."

"Same," I said. "I should've said something a long time ago."

He wet his lips, eyes grazing my body in a slow, hungry way that made my stomach flip. "Will you let me make it up to you?" His smirk illuminated a thousand promises of endless pleasure, and I swear I almost melted right then and there.

I reached for him, slowly undoing his button-down shirt, then his pants, until he matched me in just his underwear. "How about we make it up to each other?" I asked, knowing we both had a hand in this mess tonight. Both of us allowed fear to stop us from telling each other the truth.

Never again.

"Deal," he said, and his mouth was on mine, sealing the agreement with a kiss that was purely primal.

Heat spiraled down the center of me as I ran my hands over his bare chest, tipping my head back and opening for him. He swept his tongue into my mouth, curling it just the way I liked whether he was in my mouth or between my thighs. His arms snaked around me, bringing our bodies flush as he walked us backward toward the bed until we crashed against it, him holding me to his chest as we fell and never broke our kiss.

Brad rolled us to the side, slipping one thigh between my legs as his hands explored my body and mine his. We'd done this a dozen times already, but this one felt so inherently different, because this time, I wasn't questioning anything. I wasn't wondering what it meant, what this would do to our friendship, or what would happen when it all came crashing down.

Now I was able to fully lose myself in the sensations he

sparked in my body, my mind settling in the solidarity that we both loved each other, wanted each other, that this was real.

Real.

Brad was mine and I was his and there was nothing more that mattered in that moment.

I slipped my hand between us, gripping his hard length in a desperate way. "Brad," I said, stroking him. "I want you."

He grinned against my mouth, kissing me and sucking on my bottom lip. "In a hurry tonight, baby?"

I used my free hand to guide his beneath the lace I wore, slicking his fingers through my heat. "What do you think?" I whispered against his mouth.

He shuddered, a groan rippling from his chest as he took control, curling his fingers in a teasing way that made me clench with need.

"Fuck," he said, shifting us until I was on my back and he was ridding my body of the lace. "I love how needy you are for me."

I shivered as he slipped off his boxer briefs, quickly settling himself between my thighs, gliding the tip of his hard cock through my wetness. I spread myself wider for him, my heart racing when he looked down between us, watching where as he slid inside me one torturous inch.

"Look at that," he said, glancing at me. "Look how perfect you take me." He slid in another inch, and I sighed, pleasure rippling down my body at the feel of him there.

"*Brad,*" I begged, needing more. He made me hot all over, like golden fire sliding through my veins and all I wanted to do was burn.

He adjusted himself, propping himself up with an arm on either side of my head, bringing every inch of our bodies flush as he held my gaze.

"I love you," he said at the same time as he sank inside me to the hilt.

I gasped, wrapping my legs around him as he pulled all the way back our and slid home again, his pace slow, deliberate.

"I love you," I echoed his sentiment, my hands splayed on his back as he pulled out and slid in again.

And again.

He slanted his mouth over my own, kissing me with a languid, luscious pace that matched his thrusts. I arched my hips, rolling them in time to his pumping, each time we connected feeling like a silent claiming.

"You feel so damn good, baby," he groaned against my mouth, our bodies slicked with sweat from maintaining the slow pace. "So hot and slick around me. Fucking love the way your body takes mine."

"Love what you do to me," I said, barely able to form a coherent sentence as he pumped inside me, each time he bottomed out his pelvic bone ground against my throbbing clit, pushing me closer and closer to that sweet edge of release.

"We're just getting started," he said, tangling his fingers in my hair, gently tugging it back until my neck was exposed for him. "I'm going to fulfil every little desire you have, baby," he said, kissing my neck as he slammed into me a bit harder. "Whatever you want, whatever you need," he said between kisses. "Nothing is off limits."

My heart expanded at his words, my body twisting in a tight coil of heat at what he was doing to me.

"Do you like that idea?" he asked, grazing his teeth along my neck.

"Yes," I said, moaning as my pleasure built beneath my skin. "God, *yes*."

"Fuck," he groaned. "You're there. I can feel you're there, baby."

I lifted my hips as he thrust inside me, letting him slide in deeper, harder. "Come with me," I begged. "*Please*." I wanted to feel him come inside me while he unraveled me, wanted to watch him lose himself in me the same way I was in him.

"Goddamn," he said, pumping into me harder, faster, chasing his release as he stretched out mine.

I was on the cusp, each thrust adding fire to that white-hot knot pulsing inside me, just waiting to—

Explode.

I shattered into a million pieces of pleasure, sparks shooting across my skin, tightening and loosening all my muscles at once.

"*Brad*," I sighed his name as I clung to him through the intensity of my orgasm, relishing the hot burst of his release inside me.

He growled, capturing my mouth as he slowly rocked inside me, drawing out the pleasure until we were both panting and limp.After a few moments, he gently slid out of me, hopped out of the bed, and returned to clean us both up. It was loving and intimate and did all kinds of things to my heart.

He slipped back into bed, covering us both up before tucking me into his side as he wrapped his arms around me, and I wasn't sure if I'd ever be able to get used to this kind of love...

But I sure as hell would try.

CHAPTER 18

Brad

"I can't believe you're taking me to Valentine's Day dinner at Lyla's," Luna said as I held the door open for her, Anne greeting us and escorting us to our table with a warm smile on her face.

"Why wouldn't I?" I asked, genuinely confused. "It's the best restaurant in town."

Luna smiled at me from across the table, shaking her head. "I don't know," she said. "How about the fact that you proposed to Lyla right in front of me one of the last times we were here?"

I gaped at her, then clenched my eyes shut for a moment. Fuck me, I'd forgotten about that.

"That was a joke," I said, giving her my most apologetic look. "You know that."

"Do I?" she teased, the little vixen had challenge all over her. "You were so in love with her cake that day. Should I be worried?"

I cocked a brow at her, then shifted around the table, taking the seat directly next to her instead of across from her. I slid my hand over her thigh under the tablecloth, hiking it higher as I dragged my nose along her neck, stopping with my lips at the shell of her ear.

"Do you think you need to be worried, baby?" I asked, nibbling on her ear and relishing the way she instantly shifted into my touch, opening her thighs just wide enough to let my hand slide between them.

No one could see anything, thanks to the tablecloth, but fucking hell this woman was going to be the end of me. She was so open, so free, so very much *mine*.

I kissed the line of her jaw until I found her lips, kissing her like we were at home in my bed instead of our friend's very crowded restaurant. I pulled away, my fucking chest expanding at the hazy, lust-starved look in her eyes.

"What were we talking about again?" she asked, smiling up at me.

"That's what I thought," I teased, nipping her bottom lip.

We fell into an easy conversation between light kisses and eating our meals, and I did my best to not give any hint of my nerves away.

On the inside? I was an absolute mess. I'd never been attached on Valentine's Day, and I wanted it to be perfect for Luna, knowing the holiday in her past hadn't ever been an exciting one. Plus, with what I had in store for tonight, I could hardly breathe around the uncertainty of it all.

We'd only been home a few days, the retreat ending the night I almost lost her. Thankfully, I'd fixed things with Ezra and landed their investor spot, but she was way more important than any business deal. Still, I was happy to partner with them, especially when I knew their tech would only add to the success of Luna's website.

"How's Jim?" Luna asked Anne long after we'd paid the bill, the two of us stopping at the host's station to say goodbye.

"Perfect," Anne answered, motioning to a two-top table in

the back. We spotted Jim there, eating solo, and we gave him a wave. "He knew I had to work tonight, so he's determined to stay in that spot until I'm off."

"That's so sweet," Luna said, grinning at our friend.

"I can't believe you're ordering takeout on Valentine's Day," Lyla chided as she stomped out of her kitchen, eyes on Ridge who stood there with his arms crossed while he waited for his order. "Your best friend is sitting over there all alone. You could have at least stayed and eaten with him."

Ridge stared down at Lyla. "He's here for her," he said, jerking his head in Anne's direction. He leaned down, one hand on the takeout bag Lyla still held. "And if you couldn't tell, I don't give a fuck about Valentine's Day."

I cocked a brow at his rough tone, instinct telling me I should step between the two—not for Lyla's sake, but for Ridge's. Because it sure as hell looked like Lyla wanted to rip him to pieces, but I couldn't tell if it was in the fun way or send-him-to-the-hospital way.

A few heartbeats later, and Lyla's rage was replaced with a sugary-sweet look that bordered on flirtation. "That's so sad," she said, releasing the to-go order. "I'm certain the pleasure of your company would make it the most fun holiday *ever*." Sarcasm dripped from her words before she spun around, heading back into her kitchen without a glance backward.

Ridge stood there, staring at the closed kitchen door with that normal scowl on his face for a few beats before grunting and heading out the exit.

"That's always so fun to watch," Anne said, bluntly giving voice to what we were all likely thinking.

"One day she's going to tear his head off," Luna said.

"I hope so," I said, smoothing my hand over Luna's back. "It'll be funny as hell when she does."

"See you guys later," Anne said, hurrying to one of her tables before I guided Luna back to my car outside.

Nerves made my muscles clench the entire drive back to my place. It'd been as easy as choosing either her apartment or my house to stay in once we got back. Luna was still in the process of moving most of her things over. I knew everything was moving fast between us, but when I'd loved her all my life, it made a sort of sense that shouldn't make any sense at all.

And I could only hope she felt the same way as I opened the door for her and led her inside.

"You forgot something important upstairs," I said, my voice scraped raw. Fuck, why was I so worried?

"What's that?" she asked, her voice all tease. She probably thought I was about to seduce her—and yeah, I totally would —but not until after.

"I'll show you," I said, heading up the stairs toward my bedroom with her hand in mine. I let her go at the doorway, walking over to the nightstand on what was now her side of the bed. I opened the little drawer she'd claimed as hers the first night we slept here, and pulled out the ring she'd dropped inside. "This," I said, showing her the emerald engagement ring I'd given her the first day of the retreat.

She furrowed her brow, stepping further into the room. "I thought wearing it out would be in poor taste," she said, eying the ring. "Since it's not *really* mine."

I shook my head, stepping closer to her.

"This is yours," I said, then dropped to one knee, my heart in my throat. "It was never an act. Not for me. I bought this ring and could only see it on your left-hand ring-finger." I held it up to her, but she covered her mouth with her hands, her eyes wide. "I've loved you for longer than I even knew, Luna," I said, swallowing hard. "I love your mind, your body, your soul. I love the way you're a perfectionist yet chaotically creative. I love your heart and your dreams. I love the way you make me feel, which is important and needed and loved. I know this is fast, I know everything has been like a firestorm

173

with us lately, but I don't want to spend another day of my life where you aren't officially mine." I took a deep breath, reaching up and taking her left hand away from her mouth. "Will you marry me?"

I held the ring poised on the proper finger, waiting anxiously for her answer.

"Yes," she said, tears in her eyes. I slid the ring on, and she dropped to her knees, throwing her arms around me. "Yes, I'll marry you."

My heart took off like a gunshot, and I held her against me, kissing the hell out of her sweet mouth. I pulled back as we both caught our breath, and I took her left hand, raising it to my lips. "Promise me something," I said, kissing the back of her hand.

"Anything," she breathed the word.

"Don't ever take this off again," I said.

"What if I do?" she fired back, eyes dancing with challenge.

Oh, my girl wanted to play, did she? Fuck *yes*.

"You know what happens when you're my bad girl," I said, my dick already standing at attention in my pants.

She bit her bottom lip, eying the ring like she might take it off just to see. "And if I'm your good girl?" she asked, her lips inching closer to mine.

"Let me show you," I said, lightning streaking through my veins as I scooped her up and carried her to the bed.

Something I'd now have the honor of doing every night for the rest of our forever.

Epilogue

ZOE

I swear this club was pumping something through the air vents tonight. Some sort of concoction that loosened my muscles and excited my nerves.

Or it could be the mask I wore that hid my face, allowing me to be absolutely *anyone* other than the strictly professional Dr. Zoe Casson for the night.

Or it could be the dress that hugged my body in all the right ways, making me feel like an emboldened goddess rather than a mind-my-manners therapist.

Music thrummed and pulsed throughout the room, and half the dance floor was covered with my friends and their friends, most of them being Carolina Reapers. It was refreshing to see a bunch of burly, alpha hockey players masked up and letting loose, and they certainly weren't hard to look at either, but most were attached and the others already had interested parties vying for their attention, not that I was looking. I know I'd joked with Luna about pretending to be someone else tonight, but I had rules. And the first one was no one-night-stands, no matter how badly I was aching for a release. I valued structure and emotional intimacy, but something about tonight felt different. Maybe I really could be someone else.

After a few dances, I wandered toward the crowded bar in need of hydration. "Water please!" I called to the bartender once I had his attention, having had to wiggle my way in between masked bodies in order to claim a sliver of the bar.

The bartender nodded, walking toward the fridge in the back to grab me a bottle.

"You don't have to yell," a male voice said, practically right in my ear. "If you want my attention, just say so."

I turned, fully prepared to roll my eyes at the guy, but stopped short when my eyes met a whole lot of muscled chest instead of a face. I had to look up and *up* in order to see him. His face was entirely covered with a silver mask, with slits carved into it so he could see, the holes covered by some black mesh so I couldn't even make out the color of his eyes. It was intimidating as hell, but equally intriguing.

"Wasn't asking for your attention," I said, clearing my throat when it cracked slightly. He was *so* close to me, his warm, very muscled body brushing the side of mine. And sure, the entire bar was crammed in like that, but now that his attention was on me, it made me that much more aware of it.

I slid a ten to bartender once he gave me the water, and I instantly cracked it open and took a few healthy swallows. It'd been ages since I'd been to a club or dancing, and it was hot as hell in here. The water helped, and I sighed happily when I'd drained half the bottle.

"Thirsty?" he asked, his voice like liquid velvet in my ear. Jesus, were those warm chills dancing down my body because he said a single *word*?

"Why?" I asked. "You going to offer to buy me a drink?"

He tapped my water bottle with a black-gloved hand. "You

already have one," he said, looking down at me. Or at least, I think he was looking down at me. It was hard to tell with the mask. "Anything else I can offer you?"

Wow. The guy was blunt, I'd give him that. I wasn't used to that kind of directness from the past few dates I'd been on. They were all about the game, the chase, the fake details meant to make me swoon when in reality I could see right through them. It's what kept me out of the dating scene for a year— too many bad dates with too many fake people.

"I don't know," I said, adrenaline crashing through my body. Luna had said tonight was about being other people. And hell, this guy had no clue who I was. We were an hour away from Sweet Water. I could be anyone I wanted tonight. But right now, I just wanted air. "Can you become an AC for a few seconds?" I asked, fanning myself.

"Getting a little hot?" he asked, and damn him, the way he said it made me smile. There was something effortless about his voice, about the way he said things, and it was doused in a whole heap of deep, sexy tenor.

"I am, actually," I said, waving him off as I pushed away from the bar, heading toward the front doors so I could hopefully catch a little breeze and finish my water before finding my friends again.

A hand gently slid into mine, the leather from the gloves soft and buttery against my skin. I arched a brow at the masked man, but he nodded behind him before leaning down to my ear so I could hear him over the music.

"I know a cooler spot," he said.

"Is that right, Silver?" I asked, calling him by his mask's color. He certainly hadn't offered up a name, not that I had either.

Why did that excite me so damn much?

And why did I find myself keeping hold of his hand,

letting him lead me up the stairs, past the VIP balcony and up toward the roof-access door?

He held the door open for me, motioning me forward. I stepped through it, my heels immediately crunching against a graveled rooftop, complete with a lush, well-maintained garden, a scattering of wrought iron patio furniture, and a wide-open unobstructed view of the starry sky. I walked to the edge of the roof, leaning against the brick that came up to my chest, and closed my eyes as the cool breeze met my flushed skin.

"Cool enough for you, kitten?" Silver asked, his voice at my ear, the pet name likely playing on my mask which looked feline.

"It's all right," I said, shrugging like this wasn't the most romantic spot I'd ever been taken to. "Are we allowed to be up here?"

He laughed softly, his voice slightly muffled behind the full mask. "Don't worry," he said. "I know the owner. You won't get in trouble."

"Who says I'm worried about getting in trouble?" I asked, and I swear I could feel his eyes trailing the length of my body even though I had zero evidence to back that up. It was all I could do not to squirm under the silent appraisal that may or may not be happening.

"You don't look like a rule breaker," he said.

"Maybe I am," I fired back, even though he was absolutely right. Blame it on my strict upbringing, but I'd never broken any rules or stepped over any lines in the history of forever.

"Whatever you say," he said, taking up a good lean against the brick.

Jesus, even leaning he was so much taller than me, and *big*. Like muscles for days beneath the fully black clothing he wore, the gloves and outfit only adding to the mystery of his masked features. And I couldn't help it, I took my time looking at him, trailing my gaze over his muscled chest all the way down to his massive thighs. If I had to guess, I'd say the guy was an athlete, or maybe he was just a gym enthusiast.

"You're not a Reaper, are you?" I asked, suddenly curious if he'd come with the gaggle of friends Echo had brought with her.

"I don't play hockey," he said. "But I can't guarantee I won't steal your soul, if that's what you're asking."

A laugh tore through my lips, a warm shiver of delight spiraling down the middle of me at his words. At the way his presence ate up every inch of this roof even though we had miles of open sky above us. How he was somehow shaking things awake inside me that had been perfectly content sleeping before.

"Do I look that innocent?" I asked, fully committing to the little flirtation we had going.

He moved a little closer, and my heart fluttered in my chest. "Absolutely," he said. "Innocent, reserved, rule-follower. Sexy as sin, but an innocent little kitten through and through."

I parted my lips, a little flush of anger slicing through me even though he wasn't wrong. And damn it, I was *so* tired of being the things he said I was. I had been for a while, the agony of the box I'd been living in growing bigger every day.

For once, couldn't I play the part of the wild, reckless, temptress?

I could, couldn't I? I mean, that's why we were here. That's why we were hiding our identities, right? It was healthy to explore fantasies and take risks every once and a while, and I'd never done that even when I constantly advised patients to do that all the time in a safe way.

So, why not take some of my own advice?

Confidence and anticipation stormed through me.

"You've got me all wrong, Silver," I said, reaching out and

trailing a finger down his mask, shocked to find it was metal and cool to the touch instead of a flimsy plastic.

"Do I?" he asked, not drawing away from my touch. "Because something tells me one night with me and I'd ruin a perfect little thing like you."

"Who says I'm going to spend the night with you?" I asked, pulse thrumming in my veins. Excitement flared across every inch of my body.

"You did," he said, gliding that gloved hand over my bare shoulder.

I did my best not to purr at the touch.

What was it about not knowing a *thing* about this stranger —down to what color of eyes he had—that made the moment so damn sexy? Even the gloves felt forbidden against my skin, causing desire to pulse in my core in a needy little heartbeat.

What had gotten into me? Where had all my reasoning and logic gone?

I must've left them back at the bar, because I found myself asking, "When did I tell you that?"

His hand found my hip, and I let him touch me there, let him draw me closer until our bodies were flush. "The second you stepped onto this roof with me."

THE END

Don't miss Zoe's story in Sweet & Salty coming soon!

Thank you so much for reading!

New to the Sweet Water series? Check out what happens when Persephone's black sheep sister Anne comes back to Sweet Water and runs into her first love! Read Sweet & Spicy here!

. . .

Love Billionaire romance? Check out the first in my Billionaire's Game series and find out what happens when Asher Silas, the owner of the NHL Carolina Reapers, agrees to let a romance author shadow him for a novel she's working on! You can find it here!

Can't get enough sports romance? NFL quarterback Nixon Noble hasn't been able to forget—or find—the woman he spent an earth-shattering night in Vegas with...until Liberty shows up with the ultimate shock—a pregnancy test with two pink lines. Their chemistry is undeniable, but he's bound by contract, and her post-masters dream job is a continent away. Read Nixon, the first book in the Raleigh Raptors series here!

Want to start at the beginning of the Carolina Reapers? The NHL's been at Axel's door since he was eighteen, but he'd never leave the Swedish hockey league while he was raising his little brother. But now he's grown, and the Carolina Reapers are at Axel's door with his greatest weakness: Langley Pierce. The fierce and fiery publicist has sworn off men, but if she wants him to accept her proposed contract, she'll have to accept his...proposal. Read Axel, book one in the Carolina Reapers series here!

If you love these alphas and want to try something with a little more bite, check out my steamy vampire romance, Crimson Covenant!

Connect with me!

Text SAMANTHA to 77222 to be the first to know about new releases, giveaways, & more!

Text VAMPIRE to 77222 to get all the paranormal news first!

Sign up here for my newsletter for exclusive content and giveaways!

Follow me on Amazon here or BookBub here to stay up to date on all upcoming releases! You can also find me at my website here!

Acknowledgments

I want to give a MASSIVE thank you to YOU the reader. I seriously couldn't do this without you and I'm so honored that you love these series and characters as much as I do! Thank you times a thousand!

Thank you to my incredible husband and my awesome kids without which I would live a super boring life!

Huge thanks must be paid to all the amazing authors who have always offered epic advice and constant support! Not to mention creating insanely hot reads to pass the time with!

Big shout out to A.H. for making this shine. And thank you to each and every single one of you AMAZING readers who love the these books as much as I do!

About the Author

Samantha Whiskey is a wife, mom, lover of her dogs and romance novels. No stranger to hockey, hot alpha males, and a high dose of awkwardness, she tucks herself away to write books her PTA will never know about.

Made in United States
North Haven, CT
17 August 2023

40403073R00108